OTHER TEAM REAPER THRILLERS

DANGER CLOSE

A TEAM REAPER THRILLER 12

BRENT TOWNS

WOLFPACK
PUBLISHING
— EST 2013 —

Published in the United States by Wolfpack Publishing, Las Vegas

Wolfpack Publishing
6032 Wheat Penny Avenue
Las Vegas, NV 89122

wolfpackpublishing.com

Paperback ISBN: 978-1-64734-310-1
eBook ISBN: 978-1-64734-309-5

Library of Congress Control Number: 2020935687

DANGER CLOSE

CHAPTER 1

Team Reaper stepped out of the back of the Pave Hawk helicopter into the heat of western Afghanistan. The twin GE T700/701C power plants whined as the pilot wound up for immediate take off. Rotor wash blew furnace-hot air into their backs as they jogged toward three waiting Humvees. The ones in the front and back were manned by turret gunners with no unit patches on their sweat soaked BDU tops.

Kane hooked his rucksack over one big shoulder and zeroed in on the woman standing in front of the middle truck. She was the CIA liaison to the Worldwide Drug Initiative operation here in the Bakwa District of Farah province. She was the one with answers.

As he moved, the rest of Team Reaper fell in after him: Cara Billings, Axel Burton, and Carlos Arenas. Team member Richard "Brick" Peters had been pulled to work with Bravo Two, Pete Traynor, on a reconnaissance mission in northern Mexico.

Team Reaper had taken a C130 out of Fort Hood to Diego Garcia, and from there to Bagram Airfield. After spending the night in a nondescript building with a green gate controlled by the Defense Intelligence Agency, they boarded the Air Force Pave Hawk.

The helicopter ferried them to what now appeared to be the ass end of Hell.

Kane reached the liaison. She stood eight inches shorter than him, dressed in jeans and Nike cross trainers. Her red hair was pulled back in a business-like ponytail, and mirror aviator sunglasses hid her eyes. When they shook hands, her grip was firm.

"I'm Barbara Hennessey. For the record, I'm not calling you 'Reaper', just so you know."

Kane shrugged. "It's my call sign."

"Yes, well, as far as you're concerned, my call sign is 'boss'," Hennessey replied.

"Consider our balls busted," Axe said. He grinned from behind a full beard. "But can we get to the where and when, already?"

Hennessey sized him up with the disdain of a beat cop eyeing a skell. She grinned. It looked like a feral dog showing its teeth. There wasn't a lot of humor there.

"Hop in," she said.

Team Reaper climbed into the vehicle. Cara, sandwiched between Axe and Carlos, leaned over to Burton.

"Do you have to hit on everything that moves?" she asked.

"If you think that was flirting," Axe said, "then you're doing it wrong."

Cara settled back. "I never do *anything* wrong."

"Dios mios," Carlos muttered.

It sounded like a petition for patience.

Hennessey drove. She stuck her arm out the open window and pointed. Instantly, the two gun trucks fired up their engines. The little convoy took off, racing down a graded section of dirt road. Sitting shotgun, Kane looked out through the windshield. He saw a perimeter of Hesco bastions surrounding several Quonset huts and single-wide mobile homes with OD green paint jobs. There was a sandbagged pit where a howitzer crew lounged. Gun towers sat every fifty yards.

"This base doesn't feel very permanent," he said, noting the lack of amenities.

Hennessey nodded. "It started life as an Army FOB, then got farmed out to the Afghan military and our DEA as part of the Poppy Eradication program. Then the local warlord became uncooperative and made life too difficult, so they gave it to us."

"Because you straightened the warlord out?"

Carlos asked.

Hennessey laughed. It was a short, hard sound.

"No, because we had the budget to pay the bribes required to keep him in our pocket. Now it's just me, some techs from the NSA, and about half a hundred Venezuelan contractors under American leadership."

"Where do we come in?"

Hennessey pulled up to a stop in front of a Quonset hut with a reinforced roof and sandbagged walls. She shut off the Humvee. With the diesel engine quiet, Kane heard the building's HVAC system droning.

"Follow me inside and you'll find out," she said.

———————

The inside of the Quonset hut was remarkably cool after the devastating heat outside. Three intense males in civilian clothes sat at computer stations. Each area held between two and four active monitors running various programs. The techs wore headsets and typed quickly. Smart people keeping busy. Very Important Work Happening.

Kane caught Cara's gaze and she rolled her eyes at the techs and their *aren't we important* show.

Three sets of eyes looked up as they entered. Silently, Kane felt the men sizing up Reaper. Operators, door kickers, trigger pullers. Once identified and categorized, the techs returned to their screens. They murmured into their headsets like old women mumbling prayers.

To one side of the room, folding tables were set up in a U-shape around a whiteboard. An LED screen hung down from the roof, presumably to let the speaker switch between visual mediums as they made their presentation.

There was an ice chest the size of a coffin set against one wall. It was filled with Monster energy drinks and Gatorades. Hennessey pointed at the cooler as she walked past.

"Make yourself at home. Hydrate. Caffeinate up. Whatever floats your boat."

Kane hated energy drinks. He also didn't like drinking coffee in 100 plus degree weather, no matter how well the air conditioning was kicking in. That left the Monsters. He cracked one open and took a swig. Grimacing, he swallowed.

"Tastes like ass," he said. He studied the can with distaste. "Really sugary ass."

"Your diet is fascinating," Hennessey said. "It makes me miss Don't Ask, Don't Tell."

"Christ," Cara muttered. "I can't wait for our periods to sync up, we're just going to be BFFs."

"I don't get periods," Hennessey snapped. "My body fat's too low."

"I don't think that's healthy..." Carlos trailed off as both women glared at him.

"Who's flirting now?" Axe smirked.

"Fuck off," Cara said.

"Is that a PlayStation?" Carlos asked, pointing at a mess of wires and controllers on top of a familiar lump of a box.

"Don't touch it!" one of the nameless techs shouted.

"Your tax dollars at work," Axe replied.

Kane looked at Hennessey. "Maybe we can just go ahead and get started now?"

"I'm not the one who started talking about sugary asses," Hennessey said. "But I concede the point."

"Serious question," Cara said. "Where's our gear?"

"Hold all questions until the end, please," Hennessey told her.

As Reaper slid into seats, the CIA operations officer went over to the whiteboard and spun it over. On the other side topographical maps and satellite imagery were placed alongside high-resolution photographs of a compound surrounded by high mud walls.

"I know from your personnel jackets that you're prior service. I know you all have time down range. How many of you are familiar with the Taliban Red Group?" Hennessey asked.

She took off her sunglasses and set them down. Her eyes were cobalt blue. Folding her arms, she surveyed the people sitting in front of her. After a moment she took out a package of nicotine gum, punched two out from the foil, and began chewing them. She looked like a scrawny lioness masticating gristle from an old kill.

"We've been focusing on actions in the western hemisphere since inception," Kane said. "If there are new players on the ground since Operation Enduring Freedom was rolling heavy, then an overview of new players would be welcome."

Hennessey nodded. "Red Group has earned the moniker of being 'Taliban Special Forces' but that's not quite true. Basically, they're shock troops. They lead assaults, tackle tougher Afghan government forces, etc. A little like a cross between Army Rangers and a Marine expeditionary unit."

"Like the Raiders in World War Two," Axe offered.

"More or less." Hennessey nodded. "They're better trained, better paid, better equipped. They've got night vision, M4s, body armor. Frankly, they've been kicking the Afghan National Army's ass from Khyber Pass to Helmand."

"And now they're here in the west?" Cara asked.

"As part of the general international difficulties we're having with Iran, the border region has heated up recently. Except here, in the west, Taliban activity is pretty much exclusively heroin activity. A company sized element of the Red Group has moved in and taken over security of fields and transportation."

"So first we need to take them out before we can disrupt the pipeline?" Carlos asked.

Hennessey power chewed her nicotine gum. "Bingo, amigo."

"Amigo?" Carlos asked. "Was that some kind of Mexican crack?"

"You want to report me to HR?"

"What I'd like to do is—" Carlos began.

"Moving on," Kane interrupted. "Hennessey, I enjoy a good tough guy act as much as anyone, and here on the ass edge of the war I'm sure you're used to playing cowgirl, but for fuck sake, can you focus on the mission and not on trying to piss us off?"

Hennessey smacked her gum. Finally, she held up a hand and tilted it back and forth in a 'maybe' gesture.

"Dunno," she said. "If I were a Magic Eight Ball I'd have to say 'outlook is uncertain'."

"How about I bitch-slap you across the room in front of your people?" Cara asked.

"I appreciate the offer," Hennessey replied, "but I'm already seeing someone."

"For fuck sake!" Axe snapped. "What is your malfunction, lady?"

"My problem?" Hennessey grinned her humorless smirk. "It's that I've been out here for eight goddamn months building a profile on these sonofabitches," Hennessey responded. Her lips drew tight and her eyes glinted with anger. "I was promised a team of my own to roll this up, and instead I get a bunch of cops. I'm not looking to make a fucking arrest," she was almost shouting. "I'm looking to kill some motherfuckers!"

"Arrest?" Kane said.

Hennessey turned to look at him. "I'm not about due process on a goddamn battlefield."

"Hennessey," Kane said, "our code protocol is Team Reaper, not Team Miranda Warning. You wanted shooters and that's exactly what you got. Trust me, we live up to our name."

Hennessey cocked her head to one side. She studied him like it was the first time she'd laid eyes on him.

"Truly?" she asked.

"Cross my heart," Kane said.

She stared at him. There was a beat as Reaper waited to see which side of the coin Hennessey was going to land on. Finally, she grunted and then nodded once, the motion terse.

"Good enough," she said. "Are you ready to find out about your target?"

"Lady," Kane said, "we're all about finding targets."

CHAPTER 2

"I assume you're familiar with the Black Swan designation?" Hennessey asked.

Kane nodded. "Those individuals in the narcotics trade deemed too important by American intelligence to be removed. In a nutshell, anyway."

Hennessey clicked a remote, and surveillance photos of an Arabic male in his late forties filled the screen.

"Naci Sherifi Zindashtia is the Black Swan controlling the largest heroin pipeline from Afghanistan to Eastern Europe. From Albania, it crosses the Adriatic and gets in through Italy and Greece – and the Albanian Security Forces aren't beyond giving it a helping hand with the right amount of palm crossing in the silver department. I haven't been given access to what value Naci's provided to US intelligence community, or in what manner, but it was enough to give him a pass for the last five years."

"And now?" Cara asked.

Hennessey leaned forward, taking in every detail of the woman's face.

"And now he's gone and done fucked up," Hennessey said. "He's funded international terror by paying ISIS assets to mule and bodyguard shipment routes through Syria into Albania. The president pulled his Get Out of Jail Free card." She snapped her fingers. "Just that quick."

"He's here in Afghanistan?" Carlos asked.

"We don't know where he is, currently," Hennessey admitted. "That's where Team Reaper comes in. We're going to start dismantling his empire, piece by piece. At best, we'll uncover the intel we need to find him. At worst, we can turn up the heat so bad it forces him to do something stupid and reveal himself. But your hunting license is wide open. Wherever you find him you get him."

Kane grunted his approval. "So, we start here?" he asked.

Click.

The image on the screen shifted showing another Afghani male. Early fifties, full beard, bald, with a nose that had been broken numerous times.

"That's Abdul Manani, also known as 'the paymaster', and shadow governor of this province, and the man giving Red Group their orders. He runs the opium show locally. So far, he's managed to use political connections in the government and military to avoid being taken out. He had a fair amount of cover as Naci's guy. That's all changed. Our first stop is his residence right here on the borderlands."

"Opposition?" Kane asked.

Click.

The image shifted to an aerial view of a compound. Three buildings surrounded by an eight feet tall mud wall. There were several white pickup trucks and what looked like a Mercedes sedan parked inside the enclosure.

"He's got a squad of Red Group as a personal security detail. Beyond that there's usually about a platoon sized element of locals guarding the place."

"Usually?" Carlos asked.

"We have an RQ-Seven Shadow circling now," Hennessey said. She turned toward one of the three men at the computer stations. "Markus," she called, "what's our count now?"

"Twenty-eight hostiles plus the eight-man security detail."

Cara did the math. "Thirty-six shooters on the ground? Behind fortifications?" She whistled.

"Armament?" Kane asked.

"Usual. AKMs for the Taliban locals, M4s for Red Group. There are two DShK vehicle mounted machine guns. They've utilized RPG-sevens in the past."

"Collateral individuals?" Carlos asked. "Family?"

"Manani keeps a house in Kabul. His wife and children are there." She paused a moment. When she continued, her face wore an expression like she was smelling something foul. "You are, of course, aware of *Bacha bazi?*" she asked.

Kane felt the bitter taste of disgust coat his tongue. The rest of Reaper looked like they were going to vomit. "Yeah," he said. "We know."

Bacha bazi meant "boy play" and was basically institutionalized pedophilia deeply ingrained in the regional culture. The Taliban had put a stop to it during their time in power, but it had reemerged rapidly. A large percentage of green-on-blue (the designation for attacks by Afghani security forces against US Military personnel) were attributed to disputes about this practice. It was a deep and abiding regret to Kane that US Forces had turned a blind eye to the practice in the past, believing it was a local law enforcement issue, rather than *a shoot the offending fuckers through the fucking head* issue.

"Manani enjoys high status as a warlord," Hennessey said. "He keeps an SUV with five 'dancing boys' with him at all times. Other than them, it's basically a military compound."

"We can't 'hey-diddle-diddle, right-up-the-middle' against those walls," Axe said. "We need to hit him while he's on the move."

"I presume you've been tracing his routes?" Cara asked.

"Bet your ass we have." Hennessey nodded. "I've prepped strike plans for an area I think is perfect, though I have three back up contingencies."

"Let's see what you got," Kane said. "No sense reinventing the wheel."

They began planning the take down.

———

The landscape of western Afghanistan was arid and mostly barren of vegetation. It was a land of rocky hills, shale outcroppings, with dust the gray-brown color of old peanut shells. Route 515 cut through the Bakwa district. The road was packed gravel and scribed an ugly tan scar across the face of the desolate topography.

Poppies grew at higher elevations and were generally farmed there. But the 515 was a major pipeline to Iran. Reaper deployed in a low-key manner. They left the CIA base, kitted up in the early morning hours and travelled by vehicle to the kill site.

The terrain consisted of a series of low, rocky hills to the east overlooking the road. Below, a natural choke point was forced onto the route where a cement bridge dating back to the Soviet occupation crossed the shallow ravine of a dry creek bed.

Overhead the sky hung low with clouds the color of old steel. It was hot and humid, the air hanging close. There was a smell of coming rain in the air.

Reaper team presented an L-shape formation. The base consisted of Axe setting up a sniper hide on a hillock facing down the road. He pulled secondary duty as the security element. To his left, about one hundred meters away, the rest of Team Reaper formed the primary attack element. The secondary security element for the strike was the CIA Shadow UAV. It circled at its maximum flight ceiling in a loose oval pattern, providing Hennessy information she then conferred with Kane.

The approaching weather was problematic. In the manner of deserts everywhere, when it rained in Farah it came on sudden, dumped hard, causing flash floods across ground too hard to absorb moisture, and then ceased abruptly. The rain wasn't good for the Shadow. It could fly above the storm, but then its optics wouldn't benefit the team.

All of Team Reaper wore heavy duty throat microphones operating on bone conduction and plugged into tactical two-way radios. Because of a repeater in the trunk of their vehicle, signal boost wasn't a problem.

Kane spoke. "Hades, this is Reaper. Reaper in position, over."

Hennessey's voice answered back in their ear jacks. "Reaper, this is Hades, good copy, over."

"Reaper out."

"Hades out."

Reaching down Kane clicked over to the team channel. "Axe, you good?"

"Five by five, Reaper," Axe answered.

They settled in to wait with the patience of experienced hunters. In the end, this was their bread and butter: man tracking. You got a target. You took the target down and exploited any intelligence. That gave you another target. You took that target down. Rinse, repeat.

Kane clicked back over, patiently waiting for Hennessey to give them an update. He was armed with an HK16/203 combination. After the Pyros Small Tactical Munition dropped from the UAV to initiate the ambush by taking out the lead truck, he was going to fire a 40mm HE round into the rear vehicle, hopefully knocking it out and creating a book ended kill zone with the narco-terrorists trapped in the middle.

Beside him Cara deployed an M249 Squad Automatic Weapon. Her job was to rake the rear turret gunner and vehicle after the initial grenade blast. Axe's job was targets of opportunity using the M110 CSASS with a Nightforce 2.5-10X24 NXS optic system.

The sniper rifle was most commonly used by Cara, and the former Marine most frequently filled in Reaper's designated defensive marksman role during Team Reaper operations. In this case, Kane felt it would be beneficial in having a female present when it came time to shepherd the victimized children. Axe was a lot of things. Kid-friendly wasn't necessarily one of them.

That left Carlos free to use his own HK416 on the driver of the black SUV said to contain the warlord's "dancing boys". They were going to roll this thing up by the numbers. End of story. Home by dinner.

Thirty minutes dragged by. Then Hennessey's voice broke the silence even before a dust cloud appeared on the horizon.

"Look alive, Reaper," she said. "Target inbound. Hades over."

"Good copy," Kane answered. "Target inbound. Reaper out."

For thirty tense seconds nothing changed. Then, from the north east, dust clouds rose in brown ribbons like a tattered flag. Kane eased his thumb up, found the fire selection switch, and clicked it off safety. His heart beat strong but steady like a metronome.

"What do you see, Axe?" he asked on the tactical channel.

"I have the douche-canoe's entire entourage," he answered. "Three gun trucks, white Toyota pickups with Soviet crew on weapons in the back, two in front, one bringing up the rear. Third in line is our primary in a black Mercedes Benz. Behind that is the SUV with, what I assume, is his travelling kiddie creeper playground."

"Copy," Kane replied. "Team Reaper, wait for the Shadow to initiate contact. It goes without saying, but I'm going to say it, anyway; control fire around the SUV. Out."

They watched the convoy come into sight, speeding toward them. Kane glanced up at the sky even though he knew the drone circled at too high an altitude for him to see it.

"Is it too late to take a piss break?" Cara asked, her voice calm as she joked.

"A bit," Kane replied.

Below them the convoy drew close enough for them to hear the vehicles' engines.

"Target painted," Hennessy broke in. "Prepare for splashdown."

Moments later the lead gun truck crossed the bridge. A heartbeat after that the shit show began and everything went to hell.

CHAPTER 3

Kane settled in behind his sights, cheek forming a tight weld with the butt stock. Out of his peripheral vision a dark blur streaked in. The Pyros missile, formally deployed under the designation Small Tactical Munition, was 13 pounds, delivering a tight blast radius of only 5 meters. It'd been specially designed for the War on Terror in hopes of delivering pin-point strikes with minimum collateral damage.

The round slammed into the front gun truck.

It failed to detonate.

The round struck the front hood of the pickup and crushed it like a beer can. Kinetic energy shattered the windshield and tore through the vehicle occupants. Even without an explosion the force was enough to rip their limbs from their body in mushy sprays of blood and liquefied flesh.

Tires popped off the vehicle like champagne

corks. The turret gunner was thrown clear then immediately run over by the second truck speeding behind the first.

"Fuck me!" Cara said, her voice loud with amazement.

Despite the surprise Reaper operated on automatic pilot. Even as their minds struggled to comprehend the screw up that'd just occurred, muscle memory carried them through the attack.

Kane assessed distance using the grenade launcher sights and triggered the M203. The 40mm HE round arched up as recoil drove the butt of his carbine back into his shoulder. The grenade smashed into the engine block of the second truck and exploded.

Smoke billowed as the truck stopped dead, the engine block a lump of melted slag driven down into the earth. The rolling smoke cleared, and he saw the windshield in spider-webbed tatters. Both the driver and passenger were slumped loosely, painted in their own blood.

Beside him Cara opened up with the SAW, firing a long Z-pattern burst that punched a line of 5.56mm slugs across the chest of the rear turret gunner. The man jerked and flopped before pitching over the side of the truck and bouncing off the ground.

Further down, Carlos placed a tight series of semi-automatic fire into the front windshield of the SUV carrying the warlord's dancing boys. From training he knew it took upwards of six rounds with NATO standard green tip 5.56mm to penetrate ballistic glass. The key was keeping the rounds in a tight enough pattern that subsequent rounds could vector in through the breach unimpeded.

Carlos executed the technique with precision marksmanship.

Teflon coated rounds numbers 8, 9, 10, and 11, burned into the driver, shattering his sternum like a dinner plate and bouncing around inside his torso with buzz saw frenzy. Avulsions and furrows ripped through the internal organs, killing him instantly. As the man slumped, he pressed the accelerator and the SUV crashed into the stone railing of the bridge hard enough to deploy the airbag.

From the southern exposure Axe fired out of his overwatch position, executing targets of opportunity. On the kill ground everything was chaos. Red Group militants not killed in the initial strike tumbled from the vehicles.

Reaper opened up, careful to keep their fire clear of the SUV.

"Cover me while I move!" Carlos shouted.

"Covering!" Kane and Cara answered simultaneously.

On the road one of the fighters scooped up a DShK machine gun thrown clear during the initial strike. Miraculously, it functioned. Turning, he raked a ragged burst toward the hill where the Reaper attack element had taken position.

A hail of 12.7mm rounds hammered across them. Cara and Kane ducked below the slight defilade as the metal storm swept past. Carlos, scrambling to get an angle on the milling fighters, took rounds through his right leg, triceps and shoulder.

The meaty *thwacks* of the bullet impacts were clearly audible. He shouted in agony and went to the ground. Seeing the man fall, a Red Group fighter zeroed in on him. Axe put a round through the side of the man's head. A blood halo misted as the skull burst apart and the heavy gun went quiet.

The bombed lead gun truck's gas tank had ripped like old paper under the impact of the inert ammunition. Gasoline ran out into the dust like blood from a wound. From behind the wreck a Red Group fighter aimed controlled bursts at their position with an AKM.

Kane indiscriminately sprayed the back of the vehicle. All he needed was a single spark or ballistic friction through a pocket of gas. It wasn't difficult to achieve. The vehicle went up immediately with a hard, oxygen sucking *whompf* of fire and black smoke. The Red Guard stumbled screaming into the road, lit up like a Roman candle.

Bang. Kane put him down.

For a minute there was only the sound of raging

car fire. Reaper scanned the ambush site, looking for any sign of movement. There was nothing down there but bullet riddled wrecks and bullet riddled bodies. The black SUV sat untouched except for the holes over the driver's side seat.

Behind him Carlos tried not to groan, but the wounds had come fast and hard. Kane saw Cara begin administering first aid. She dumped coagulation powder onto Carlos' leg with practiced, economic motions.

Suddenly, Carlos shuddered and went limp. His head lolled as he fell unconscious. Grimacing, but knowing he was in good hands, Kane turned back to the mission.

"Let's sweep through, Axe," Kane said into his throat mic.

"Copy," Axed answered. "On my way."

"Out," Kane signed off.

"Delay that, I need help!" Cara shouted at him. "He's stopped breathing!"

Instantly Kane went over and knelt beside the inert form of Carlos as Cara used a size-3 Macintosh blade on a Paramedic Laryngoscope to intubate the unconscious man. Sliding the flexible plastic tube down Carlos's throat she then secured an OD Green bag-valve-mask to the slack muscles of his face.

"I can't get a peripheral pulse. Compressions," she instructed. Without hesitation Kane used his boot knife to cut Carlos from his body armor, then found the appropriate spot on his sternum and began performing CPR chest compressions.

He turned his chin into one shoulder, keying the throat mic. "Axe, change of plans. Fall in here to provide cover."

"Copy," Axe replied.

Kane worked steadily as Axe made his way over at a dead run.

Cara crushed the rubber balloon of the bag-valve-mask under her hand, forcing fresh oxygen into Carlos' lungs. Kane went to work pushing down on the sternum hard enough to snap cartilage.

"People!" Cara snapped. "I need another set of hands."

Coming up to them, Axe taking the BVM from her.

"Slow," she reminded him; "one, two, squeeze. Quick and hard. Stay calm."

Axe nodded his understanding, operating the BVM with steady hands. "How far is he gone?"

"He's got no circulation. I hope the heart stopped because his lungs couldn't get the O2 it needed, and not the other way around. I need to use my drugs."

Even as he explained the situation her hands were in motion. "I'm pushing an amp of Epi in now. Keep pumping hard, Reaper! I need to be able to find his veins without a central line."

Kane responded with renewed vigor. "I can feel his heart beating under my hands! But it feels funny," he stopped, searching for some way to describe what he was experiencing. "Like a rabbit running zig zag jumps," he said finally.

Cara just nodded as she pulled the Epi syringe clear. "V-fib. Christ, I wish we had an automated defibrillator out here." She reached into her medic kit and pulled out another pre-filled syringe. "I'll use lidocaine," she said out loud, more to center herself than anything else.

Kane watched her feed the drug into a vein in Carlos' forearm. Technically, he knew, the ex-Special Forces operator was already dead. Without help and access to advanced medical care, he silently held little hope the man would make it.

"Pushing another two amps of Epi," Cara said.

Again, it was mostly to herself she spoke as she injected the adrenalin straight into Carlos' system for a second time. Kane continued pushing compressions as she administered the drug, and for several moments after she finished he couldn't detect a change. Carlos's skin had gone very gray.

Carlos's eyes came open and he sucked in a breath. It was wet and ragged and sounded more like a choking gasp than anything, but he was alive.

Kane smiled in relief. He squeezed Carlos' hands and nodded to him. In the next moment he stood, weapon ready. He nodded to Axe.

"Let's roll this up while Cara alerts Hades to the medical situation."

Nodding, Axe rose, weapon in hand, and began sidestepping down the loose gravel on the hill, circling toward the front of the convoy. Kane went over the three-foot cliff face beneath the ambush position and skip-ran down through clumps of dry cheatgrass toward the road.

Cara's voice broke squelch, "Hades, one for medevac, repeat, one for medevac."

"Copy, inbound," Hennessey immediately replied.

Axe came out just behind the rear vehicle in the convoy and began slowly walking up the line, weapon ready. This part of combat always fascinated him on some morbid level. There was the endless, broken-clock waiting leading up to the fight, there was the chaos of battle, and then in a moment, it was simply over. You helped the wounded; you saw blood pooling around spent shell casings. One heartbeat everything was fire and fury, the next stillness.

Walking up to the rear vehicle he checked a dead fighter, saw fixed and dilated pupils staring blankly toward the Afghanistan sky, and stepped over him. He stood at an angle to the door and brought up his weapon. Using his other hand, he tried the door, found it unlocked, and swung it open.

He checked the vehicle. Death and destruction,

nothing lived. Pulling out of the truck he looked down the line and saw Axe, weapon ready, approach the untouched black SUV. They made eye contact and Axe nodded.

Kane was on the ground. He couldn't hear and he didn't understand what had just happened. Pushing himself to his feet his ears started ringing in a cacophony. He brought his weapon up, confused as a drunk at last call. He blinked his vision into focus. He tasted dust and blood in his mouth. The stench of cordite hung in the air.

The black SUV was blown apart. On fire, it poured foul black smoke up in a column. Kane couldn't remember it blowing up. One second, he and Axe–

Axe! he thought.

"Axe!" he shouted. "You okay, brother? Axe!"

He didn't know if the SUV had been primed to blow, if someone inside had worn a suicide vest, or if some outside actor had struck the vehicle with some sort of explosive round. He swept out in a circle, scanning the area, looking for sign of Axe.

He caught motion out of the corner of his eye and half turned, saw who it was, and turned back to the burning wreckage.

Cara came down the hill fast. She was saying

something, and Kane realized he still wasn't hearing correctly because her voice sounded like it was coming from underwater. He worked his jaw trying to pop his ears and continued looking around.

He saw a pair of familiar boots sticking out onto the side of the road where a shallow depression had been formed on the side of the road. He ran forward, the rest of the body came into view and he saw it was Axe. Automatically, he triaged him as he approached.

Kane couldn't tell if he was still breathing but all of his limbs were attached. His hand found his radio as he jogged forward.

"Two down, Hades," he said. "Two down, roll Medevac."

"I copy, Reaper," she answered immediately. "We're less than five klicks from your position."

He didn't bother listening to the reply. Reaching Axe, he dropped to one knee and felt the unconscious man for a pulse. It was there, weak and fluttering, but present. He began doing a rapid physical assessment. His hand blindly groped for trauma shears secured in a sheath-like pouch in the middle of a large cargo pocket on his pants.

Cara came up and grabbed him by the shoulder. His ears popped and her words rushed in.

"Go!" she said. "I got this, pop smoke to bring the chopper in."

"Roger," he muttered.

His head cleared and he was on his feet. He realized the explosion must have rattled his brain around inside his head pretty damn hard, but he was coming out of it.

I better not end up with a goddamn TBI, he thought. Traumatic Brain Injuries were terrifying prospects. Too many good brothers had had their lives changed forever by them.

He jogged forward, heading off the bridge toward a stretch of level ground between two rocky hillocks they'd picked out as an LZ during planning. Unclipping a smoke grenade from his web gear he popped it and chucked it down so the pilot could gauge wind position and speed as they approached.

He eyed the devastated convoy as the sounds of a Blackhawk came over the horizon. It was a mess of burning, mangled devastation and smoke. Reaper was in little better shape, he grimly realized.

Wherever the fuck you are, Naci, he thought, *I'm coming to get you.*

Kane couldn't sleep.

Both Carlos and Axe had been lifted to Bagram. Carlos was doing well after surgery. Axe hadn't woken up yet. He tried going over the events, to second guess himself, but too much of the time right when the explosion happened was gone, a black void in his memory.

Reaper had been reaped.

Live by the sword, die by the sword, he thought.

He wasn't much given to biblical quotes. At times his belief in an invisible sky father was sorely tested by the horrors he witnessed, by the evil men did. In the end though, his faith, as nonspecific as it often was, was much a part of his dogged self-identity as his patriotism. He fought on behalf of his countrymen for his country. Acknowledging there were things larger than himself was a big part of it.

"Holy shit," he muttered. "I must have had my bell rung to start philosophizing at a time like now."

"What's that?" Cara asked.

"Nothing," Kane replied.

Cara sat across the room, pouring coffee into a paper cup. She used a red plastic swivel stick to stir in some powdered creamer. She took a drink, made a face, set the cup down in disgust.

The two of them were alone.

"I don't feel like I should have to say this," Cara said. "You've got more time down range than I do–"

"You've seen plenty of combat," Kane interrupted.

Cara shook her head. "Not the point. And I certainly haven't led as many people into operations as you have."

Kane started to say something, and Cara made a

short, sharp chopping motion with her hand.

"Listen to me, you stubborn jarhead, deal?"

Kane grunted, but relaxed into his chair.

"Ops go bad," Cara said. "That didn't go bad because our tradecraft sucked, or you made bad calls. It went bad because our intel was bullshit. Carlos knows that. And when Axe wakes up, he'll say the same. Operations aren't fun thrill rides where everyone goes unscathed. It's not a goddamn extreme sport."

"I know that," Kane growled.

"Then shake it off and put your eyes on the prize," Cara scolded.

The corner of Kane's mouth tugged upward, as if threatening to break into a grin.

"And prize we have, my little -chick-a-dees!" Hennessey said.

She came into the room like an anorexic cyclone. She held a vape in one hand and the smell of lavender scented tobacco preceded her into the room. In her other hand she held a pile of printouts. Her eyes had the excited gleam of a religious zealot or a coke addict, and she was smiling. Her orange red hair frizzed out around her face like springs poking through the fabric of an old couch.

"*Found* the sonofabitch," she half chortled, half snarled.

She slapped the paperwork she held down. Kane looked. The manila folder holding everything was stamped SPECIAL ACCESS PROGRAM Ebony Drake.

"The paymaster?" Cara asked.

"Give the woman a kewpie doll," she crowed. "We have a site address in Farah," she said. "Pulled it straight off a cellphone secured at the ambush."

She picked up a remote and hit the power on a HD wall mount television. It showed Farah province with the city marked. It was on the border of Iran and positioned next to the Farah River. There was a US base positioned at the airport.

"Farah's the capital of the province," she informed them. "Population a bit over one hundred thousand. Only last year Taliban forces had captured and held the city for two days. Combined US and Afghan forces drove them out but the damage to infrastructure was tremendous."

"Chaos?" Cara asked.

"Yeah," she said. "You could say that. The resurgent Taliban are in the middle of an offensive. They control parts of the southeast. Especially along the river."

"Great," said Axe. "That's really going to help."

"Smugglers paradise," Kane said. "Large population to blend into, ineffective law enforcement. A border close by."

"Right," Hennessey nodded. "Admittedly, there's no direct road connection to the border. But the Farah River goes right down into the Helmand swamps on the Iran border."

"No road," Cara said. "The US controls air traf-fic exclusively."

"That leaves the river," Kane finished.

"Now you're cooking with gas," Hennessey said.

———————

The land around the river held the heat of the day even as twilight lengthened into night. By eleven it was well and truly dark and what was left of Team Reaper began their operation. The river was a stinking, polluted mess and at the shoreline the mud was noxious with industrial waste, oil, and leaked gasoline. Kane doubted strongly the fish caught here were any kind of edible.

Hennessy guided the boat down the river with an experienced hand. The craft was a Boston Whaler Montauk running a 90 hp Mercury engine. It looked beat to shit and boasted grimy green fish-ing nets off the prow but that was just part of its cover, Kane noted. The engines purred.

The CIA officer knifed the boat across a runnel of chop and powered down the Mercury. Cara sat up front, Mk 18 in a narrow gear locker at her feet. She wore a black hijab to avoid announcing her presence as a Western female and a light jacket over her vest and shoulder rig. Kane also wore neutral color civilian clothes.

As they approached a cement pier Hennessey cut the engine all together and coasted into a narrow slip. The prow nudged into place, cushioned by the nets and came to rest. Kane and Cara rose and scrambled up onto the pier. It ran alongside a dilapidated storage shed made of corrugated tin.

Once they were off, Hennessey made eye contact with Kane. The big Marine nodded. The Mercury purred to life and pulled away back into the river. The two Reaper operators moved a few yards down the weather-beaten cement to the edge of the warehouse and stood beside a stack of old tires.

They waited patiently for several minutes, listening to the drone of the Boston Whaler fading into the distance. They didn't speak as they waited to catch the rhythm of the city around them. The waterfront was a bustling place during the day, but under military curfew it was deserted this time of night.

There was the sound of traffic, but it was distant, blocked by buildings. A battered looking street dotted with sodium lamp streetlights ran past lines of rundown industrial buildings and commercial warehouses. Every structure stood silent and dark.

It was past curfew. Any people out would be as eager to avoid contact as the Reaper duo were. Not counting authorities. A large portion of which were corrupt.

A rat climbed up a slimy old mooring rope and

looked at them.

"You take me to all the best places," Cara said.

Kane chuckled. "You get to use your favorite accessories."

Cara nodded and patted her shoulder-holstered pistol. "When you care enough to send the very best," she agreed.

Kane checked down the street, scanned roof tops. He nodded to himself, satisfied.

"Can I interest you in a little B&E?"

"Absolutely," Cara replied.

They crossed the street at a quick pace but not running. They entered the dark chute of a narrow alley and blended into the shadows. They passed piles of old pallets, empty 55-gallon drums, and several overflowing dumpsters. Halfway down they came to a door set in the building at the bottom of a short staircase.

Cara removed her SIG Sauer M17 and held it down by her leg. Kane slipped the lockpick gun into the keyhole and pulled the lever. With a muted *snap* the bolt clicked back. He opened the door and they slipped inside.

———————

They crouched at the end of a short, dark corridor. Weapons ready they slid down the hallway toward a door at the end. This was a heavy, steel fire door, but unlocked. Once through it they found themselves in the warehouse. What Kane took to be several dozen vehicles sat under tarps. There was a winch-hoist on a track overhead and several mechanic jacks lined the wall.

The place smelled like old grease and dust. The cement under their feet was cracked with age. Waiting for a moment to ensure they were undiscovered they surveyed the interior. To the back stood several open large roll up bay doors leading to the loading docks. There was a sliding door on rollers and a track in the front. It took up about a third of the front wall of the building.

Directly across from them a set of scaffolding stairs lead up to a bare-bones mezzanine where some boxy rooms with windows overlooking the floor stood. There was a light on in one of the windows.

A radio played somewhere, turned low. The vast acoustics of the place distorted the sound so they couldn't tell where it came from. It played traditional Afghani folk music with sitars and rubabs.

Kane nodded. They split apart, darting through the cars toward the metal steps. Kane shifted his muzzle, scanning the catwalk-like structure. Beside him Cara edged up and quietly hissed for his attention.

He looked over. She indicated the floor to their left with her chin. He looked over and frowned.

5.45mm shell casings lay on the floor. There were about twenty. Crouching he touched one in the center.

"Still warm," he murmured.

"You can still smell cordite," Cara whispered.

"Nitro," corrected Kane. Pungent nitroglycerin had replaced cordite in shells somewhere near the end of WWII. "How many times…?"

"Ok, Mister Big Brain. Nitro."

"Best to be accurate. Now stay *sharp.*"

They climbed the stairs. Even though they went slow, each step threatened to reverberate up the metal structure, and they put their feet down carefully. Kane covered the catwalk above them while Cara watched their six. It took several minutes to reach the top. They slid toward the office entrance heel-toe, heel-toe. As they got closer, they saw the particle board door was riddled with bullet holes. The knob was missing, perhaps carved off by automatic fire or blown at close range with a shotgun.

The smell of nitro was heavier here.

Kane looked at Cara. She nodded pistol ready. He pushed the door the rest of the way open. It swung in on flimsy hinges, revealing the gloomy office. Kane snapped his muzzle through the vectors, clearing quickly then stepping inside, taking the room more like a cop would than a Marine infantry squad.

Bullets had flown through the door and then

the far back wall. A cork board was set up and it had been chewed apart, papers pinned there were perforated and shredded. Holes the size of 50-cent pieces dotted the wall.

In front of the corkboard was a nondescript desk. It'd taken only five or six rounds. An older model table station PC had been blown apart. The remains of the exploded monitor sat in splinters on the desk. The chair was overturned.

Under the windows overlooking the warehouse floor was a grimy linoleum counter. There was a cheap coffee maker on it, untouched. No bullets had struck the window. Several dirty coffee cups lay overturned next to the pot.

The place was empty.

"Lot of shooting, no blood," Cara said.

Kane grunted. He went over to the desk and began rifling the drawers. Cara went back to the doorway and scanned the warehouse, covering the team six. She heard Kane give a soft exclamation.

"That's special," he said.

She looked at him. "What?" she asked.

He grinned. "You're going to have to see for yourself."

She walked over and peeked around him.

In the base of the top drawer sat a huge brown spider under a squat black candle. She jumped back, startled. The spider sat there. She squinted into the gloom then looked at Kane.

"You're a fucker," she said.

"Trying to keep the magic alive."

The spider was a severed human hand.

The candle had been melted into the palm and jutted up like a street sign. The hand itself was old and withered to the point of desiccation. On the back of the hand, near the base of the thumb closest to the first finger, there was a faded green teardrop tattoo.

"What is that?" Kane grunted. "Some kind of fucking voodoo?"

"Are Hands of Glory part of Islamic folklore? I thought it was strictly European spooky dark witchcraft stuff."

"Hand of Glory? I know I've heard that...but what the hell is it?"

Cara shrugged. "Take a bad criminal, hang him. As he sways back and forth all dead and stuff you: One; cut off his left hand. Two; take his fat and turn it into candle tallow; and Three; cut his hair to make a wick."

Kane made a face, "Burnt hair? Screw that. Okay so I get the funky Black Mass construction, but what is it *for*? Is it a warning, like mob guys sending a fish?"

Cara looked nonplussed. "*Godfather* is not the greatest movie ever made."

"Is."

"Isn't."

"Is."

"Really?" Cara asked. Is this how we're going to pull ops now?"

Kane scowled. "You started it." He held his hand. "This place feels like it's full of clues for Sherlock Holmes, but not stuff intel can use, and not with our bad guy. Does the purpose of a Hand of Gore—"

"Glory."

"–Glory, like I said, maybe mean something here?" he finished.

Cara shook her head, frowning. "I don't see how. The legend is that it could open any lock. I get that there's metaphorical connotations to 'opening locks' but I don't see how it'd work in a narco-terror organization. Maybe Mexican Cartels, because of Santa Muerte worship, but not over here."

Santa Muerte translated to "Our Lady of Death," and was a hybrid of Catholicism focused on death imagery, among other things. It had nothing to do with Afghanistan in any way.

"Then Whiskey Tango Foxtrot, over," Kane said.

"Occam's Razor," said Cara. "The simplest solution is usually best."

"Which means?"

She shut the drawer. "That they're a bunch of freaks and should be taken out ASAP."

"*Oorah.*" Kane nodded. He stopped, held up a hand to silence further talk. After a moment he asked, "You hear that?"

Cara cocked her head, concentrating. She looked up and met his eyes. "The music's stopped."

They weren't alone.

They dropped into a crouch. As they already knew, the walls of the office would stop bullets. Someone below them firing blindly with the right weapon could finish them off. Kane moved in a crouch to the door. Staying low he unobtrusively scanned the dark building below them.

Down in the gloom he saw movement. He pointed his fingers at his eyes then down to the floor, Cara nodded in understanding. Tense, they watched a strange procession emerge up out of cellar doors set in the floor.

"That doesn't look good," Cara whispered.

The figures wore traditional garb of robes and shemagh headpieces. Scarves obscured their faces. If the Paymaster was with them, there was no way to identify him. Without speaking they made their way to the largest tarp-covered shape. It was a beat-up Toyota van painted white.

The group opened the backdoors and pulled out a bound and hooded figure. The figure hung limp.

"Nope," Kane agreed. "Doesn't look good."

"The stairs are too exposed."

Below them the figures threw the captive down and ripped off the black hood covering his face. He was Afghani, in his thirties, portly, and his face showed signs of prior beatings. Dried blood painted his mouth like lipstick.

Kane looked up. Steel girders formed rafters below the warehouse roof. He scanned the ceiling, following the connecting lines of the cross pieces. Right above the office structure two of the metal struts were barely three feet above the roof.

He pointed. Cara looked. She looked dubious then shrugged. There were no good options.

Below them the majority of the group began working at some kind of task while two of the men watched the prisoner. They took turns kicking him.

Cara holstered her sidearm and stood in the office door. As Kane covered her, she did a slow pull up and eased over the edge onto the structure's ceiling. Dust lay thick and his front was covered in it. She crouched in the shadow of the strut and drew her firearm again.

"Go," he subvocalized.

Below them four of the group were pinning a large black flag with white Arabic writing on the wall. Two more assembled a video camera and tripod. One man stood a little apart from the figures, directing the work of the others.

You die first, Kane thought.

As Kane covered her, Cara eased onto the girder. It was a little larger than a 4x4" post and made out of cold rolled steel. The joists ran at parallel intervals, connected by numerous crosspieces. Cara eased forward, moving slowly to accommodate the fact they held their pistols ready.

After the tripod mounted camera and large flag were positioned, the lone figure barked several orders. The guards dragged the manacled prisoner over and sat him on his knees in front of the flag. The chained man didn't struggle. One of the figures stepped up. Opening his robe, he drew a large sheath knife from inside.

As Cara crawled closer, they heard the men laughing. There was a bit of a party atmosphere going on, Kane observed. He watched Cara inch into position over the group. Taking aim, he waited. There was a long moment where the only sound was the shrill declarations of the man wielding the knife.

A canister a little smaller than a can of beer dropped into the knot of people clustered behind the camcorder. Kane knew she was in motion to drop a second one. He double tapped his pistol at thirty yards. He could maintain a two-inch grouping at that range and placed both .40 caliber rounds in the leader's chest.

The flash-bang went off with a thunderclap. A line of brilliant orange-red light strobe-lit the area. Men screamed at the cacophony and staggered. The second one went off hard on the heels of the first. Kane opened his eye and re-centered his vision. Cara began firing downward into the confused crowd of terrorists.

He aimed at a stumbling figure and pulled the trigger twice. The man jerked and fell. Shifting slightly, he drew up his sights and killed another one. The designated executioner jerked and stutter-stepped as Cara's rounds hammered home. Seizing his opportunity, the prisoner leapt to his feet and used his handcuffed hands to rip the hood free.

He looked Afghani from Kane's vantage. His hair was thickly-tousled black and his mustache slim to the point of being dapper. Unlike his captors, he was beardless. He looked around, obviously terrified.

"No, no, no," Kane said to himself. The guy was going to bolt.

A terrorist appeared next to the man. Kane shot him at the same time as Cara. The prisoner raced for the door. Kane holstered the pistol and dove for the stairs. He came down them fast, all pretense at stealth left behind. Cara was relentless from the rafter, killing the figures without mercy. The floor of the factory was starting to look like the intake chute in a slaughterhouse.

He didn't see what caused Cara to fall.

Kane caught a flash of motion out one eye and spun toward it. He turned in time to see her hit the ground, limp as a rag doll. He winced at the *thump* her body made.

"Cara!" he shouted.

He gut-shot the last terrorist then put two rounds through his head as the man fell. Even as the echoes of his rounds reverberated off the warehouse walls he was on the move. She was unconscious. A pool of dark blood grew, spreading from out behind her head.

He looked toward the prisoner. The man, still handcuffed, reached the big doors and began trying to yank one open. He fired a single round, burning it over the man's shoulder and putting it into the sliding door.

"Freeze!" he barked. "Come here or the next one kills you."

The obviously terrified man held his cuffed hands up and began shuffling toward Kane. Kane risked a look at Cara. She didn't look good. He swallowed. This whole operation felt cursed to hell and back. He'd never lost this many people ever. Seemingly everything that could go wrong had gone wrong. He felt sick to his stomach when he eyed how high above them the rafter was.

As the prisoner came closer Kane pointed his weapon at him.

"Sit!"

The man sat.

Kane took a knee beside Cara. He sighed with relief when he found a pulse but the blood pouring from her head worried him badly. Using the pistol grip, he kept the M4 trained on the man. With his other he pulled the secure sat phone free and hit the pre-coordinated speed dial.

Hennessey answered at once. Kane was actually relieved to hear her voice.

"Things went sideways," he said without pre-amble. "I got several dead tangos and a live hostage they were about to kill. I need medics now."

"I'll roll the QRF from the Army FOB," she said. "So much for low profile."

"Yeah," Kane agreed. He clicked the phone off.

CHAPTER 4

The hostage, who'd said his name was Ardashir Rahmani, once he'd got over thinking that his head was going to be cut off, or then shot by Kane, had been more than grateful to the Reaper leader for getting him out. All the way back in the Pave Hawk, he'd babbled his thanks and his wishes that Kane and his children would live a thousand years, praise be.

When Kane had shouted at him over the *thwop-thwop-thwop* to explain why he was about to have his head cut off, and why the dead Tangos had brought him to be executed in a warehouse where the paymaster Abdul Manani, was supposed to be hanging out, Rahmani couldn't shut his mouth quickly enough. Kane thought, not unreasonably, if the ex-hostage hadn't been zip-tied ankle and wrists, dumped on the gritty and sand covered floor of the chopper, that he might have thrown himself out the door without a second thought, such was the terror in the eyes above the clamped lips.

That was thirty hours ago. Cara was out of ICU and she was going to make it.

Hennessy had handed Rahmani over to her CIA Can-Openers, as she called the practitioners of what was euphemistically known as *Enhanced Interrogation Techniques* in the same way that Boxing was euphemistically called a *Sweet Science.*

"We have...complications," Hennessey said as she came into the room. Kane had been going over the intel and chatter from all the sources he could get his eyes on. Looking for anything that might lead him to Manani and then through him to Naci. Revenge was never a good motivator when it came to going into the field, but right now, thinking about the broken bodies of his comrades, it was definitely a consideration. Kane narrowed his eyes at Hennessey.

"Complications? One day something will be easy."

"Nothing worth having ever is."

Hennessey poised herself in the edge of the desk where Kane had been cycling his screen through reports and sat images, like someone settling a particularly succulent cherry on top of a cake.

"What do you know about codename Midnight?"

"Female intelligence freelancer? Mercenary.

Gun for hire. All the moral fortitude of a bomb in an orphanage. She's worked for us and worked for them. She works for whoever has the dollars. Bet she's a fantastic dancer too. Has all the tools in the bag."

"That's the doggie, yes," Hennessey replied. "Seems Rahmani overheard a conversation by the guys who were going to relieve him of his skull that Midnight. Well he overheard her cover name, and that set off all sorts of alarms when we fed it into the system. Midnight, in her undercover guise was slated to meet them at the warehouse."

"I'd say anything if I'd been leaning with my forehead against a wall for seventeen hours and a bulldog clip on my nutsack."

"I'll write that down. Might come in useful later."

"Ha! What makes you think this just isn't the ramblings of a guy trying to ingratiate himself on your Can-Openers?"

"I'm told he was very convincing. Especially when they heard the cover name she was using."

"So, what does Midnight have to do with this?" Kane clicked off his screen and leaned back in the chair. There was no getting away from the fact that Hennessey, although thinner than an air sandwich, had something about her that that made his focus difficult to keep on one thing. The job.

"She was engaged in...work for us. Cross pollination, shall we say? She was being run out of the covert Iran station house by an analyst named Clark."

"Look, this is all very well, but what has this got to do with us and Naci?"

"Midnight had contact with the paymaster. Which is why she was meeting the head-hunters at the warehouse. They were doing a little sideline murder while they were waiting. Rahmani was suspected of being an informant, so they were teaching him an extreme lesson."

"And was he an informer?"

"Well, he is now. If he knows what's good for him."

"The paymaster was due to be there too, as we know. Didn't show. But Midnight has a lead on him."

"Ah."

"Yes, and several other letters of the alphabet too. Now, put your chin back on your face and get this. She was investigating the theft of certain schematics. Nuclear centrifuge. Enriched Uranium processes. Portability stats. All the bingos."

That got Kane's attention. He leaned forward. "Useful to the Iranians."

"Yes, or any other shit on a stick who wants to make a point to the Israelis. Or us."

"And these schematics were on their way to…" Kane was already filling in the dots.

"The paymaster, and through him to Naci. Seems like Naci wants to go up in the world. Running the huge-y-ist heroin operation in Afghanistan isn't enough for him."

"And we're only finding this all out *now?*"

Hennessey nodded. "It only came down the line to us because of what else has happened."

"Is this the complication, because I'm telling you, it all feels very complicated right now."

"We didn't know Midnight was going to this meeting because Clark, her handler, didn't tell anyone about it."

"Significant that he didn't call in through the station house," Kane said. His voice was somber.

Hennessey nodded. "I do. However, my control isn't choosing to see it that way. It's Clark that's broken protocol. Since he's the one initiating the messiness, they figure the break is just an extension of this."

"So we're going to Iran…" Kane was already on his feet. "I'll need my toothbrush."

"Yup. As far as we know, Clark isn't aware that we know he's not been entirely on the level. I figured you'd be up for a little Bond-work."

Kane snorted. "Bond is a pussy."

Hennessey said, "And there's me thinking that would make him one of your favorite things…"

Kane coughed. *Focus.* "I want to do everything I can to get an understanding of the situation before

I meet with this station head, Mundt," Kane said. "I want to operate independently for as long as possible. We'll set up a meeting with Clark."

"That shouldn't be a problem, big picture, anyway."

"There's another wrinkle? Be still my beating heart."

"Well, yes," Hennessey said. "Midnight was playing both sides, it seems. Either Clark didn't know, or he wasn't telling. So that means the Iranian internal security service is also looking for her. Our investigations could overlap; you could come to their attention. We do have access to equipment caches and safe houses though, which might help."

That changed nothing. One step closer to Clark and Midnight was another step closer to Naci.

"Okay," Kane said. "Understood. We're a go."

CHAPTER 5

Kane walked into the hotel lobby. It was cool inside out of the heat and he was uncomfortably aware of how much he was sweating. The place buzzed with activity. He crossed to a waiting area adjacent to the front desk and took a seat. He opened the newspaper he carried under his arm. It was the Edinburgh Scotsman.

He was just supposed to sit and read it. Clark would make contact and they'd trade code paroles.

The feeling of sitting there was uncomfortable. He was dressed nondescript and his beard had filled in. As unobtrusively as possible he scanned the lobby, clocking the population. He saw four or five sets of couples moving across the space. Three employees worked the desk, helping customers and answering phones. A valet lounged at a podium-kiosk, waiting for a guest to drive up.

A man across the lobby drew his eye. He was on

the youngish side, perhaps mid-twenties. His hair was a little wild and he was whipcord thin under street clothes. When he noticed Kane looking, he pulled his phone and began thumbing through apps or texting. Kane returned to his paper.

He looked up again a minute later, using the motion to check the clock set over the doors in the lobby. The schedule for the meet was a ten-minute window. If Clark hadn't made contact, then the coordination was considered aborted. When Kane looked up, he discovered the valet looking at him.

The man was husky, not as big as Kane, but over six feet and two hundred pounds. His face was full and sported a dapper thin mustache. He looked away. Growing apprehensive, Kane glanced at the clock. Five minutes to go.

He went to check for the first man and found him gone. Maybe his apprehension had been for nothing. The valet was taking a cart loaded with luggage toward the elevator bank. He looked at the clock. Clark had three minutes to show and then it was time to try and salvage something.

Kane covered his face with the paper.

"No contact, proceeding to dead drop," he said.

"Any heat?" Hennessey asked.

"Nothing for sure," he answered. "I could just be getting spooked."

"Watch your six."

"Copy."

He rose and folded the paper under his arm. Forcing himself to move in a leisurely way he strolled toward the bathrooms by the elevators. He pushed his way through and entered the men's room. Sink, urinals, three stalls, linoleum floor, and large mirror behind the sinks. He paused for a moment, checking the surroundings.

He was alone.

He walked to the last stall and entered. He sat down and inspected the toilet paper dispenser.

"I'm here," he told Hennessey. He produced a knife and opened the blade.

"Alright, good," she said. "The window for the dead drop is supposed to be two hours max, during a time they know housekeeping wasn't scheduled to clean the bathrooms. If there's anything there it means Clark hasn't been making his drop. It could provide us with some insight into who he was running as part of his op since he kept everything from Mundt."

Kane finished prizing the faceplate loose at a corner. He saw now that the area behind the plate provided a space between the metal fitting and the wall. Inside the space was a thumb-drive. He felt like a kid playing pirate and finding buried treasure.

"Bingo," he breathed.

"You found something?" Hennessey asked. He could hear the excitement in her voice.

The bathroom door opened.

"Company," Kane said.

Standing, he put the thumb drive in his pocket, flushed and left the stall.

"Company?" Hennessey repeated.

The valet and the thin kid looked at him. The valet grinned, revealing a gold tooth that gleamed dully against his olive complexion. He said something in what Kane took to be Farsi. The thin kid laughed.

"How you boys doing?" Kane said.

"Is that how guys talk to each other in the bathroom?" Hennessey asked.

Both of them made comic expressions of surprise at what he assumed was him speaking English. The valet lost his smile. He said something else to the thin kid then went over to the door and, jamming a foot against the bottom, put his shoulder against it.

The thin kid reached behind his back and pulled out a pair of nunchucks. Kane blinked. He'd been close to drawing his pistol because he took it for granted that the kid was going for one of his own.

"I'm not going to lie, fuck face," Kane said. "I really wasn't expecting that Bruce Lee stunt."

Hennessey broke in. "Yeah! Bringing up Bruce Lee is *tres* butch. Let these guys know who's the top and who's the bottom."

Kane went to growl his response, realized the two men would think he was talking to them.

The thin kid smiled, then began snapping them around. Over the shoulder, behind the back, one side to the other, figure eight, the hands twirled almost too fast to follow. He brought them to a sudden stop, one trapped beneath his arm the other holding the stick so the chain was taut.

Kane remembered the scene in Indiana Jones where the black turban assassin had twirled his tulwar around to intimidate the good Dr. Jones, who then promptly shot him. Problem was his pistol wasn't silenced. If he shot now in the echo chamber of a bathroom everyone in the lobby would hear the gunfire. He'd have to face the police and there'd be video of his face.

"Sit rep, Reaper," Hennessey said. "Are you still dicking around with those two? Get it? I said dick–"

"Shut up, Hades!" Kane barked.

He moved to one side as the thin kid slid forward and rapid fired a trio of strikes at him. Kane just managed to avoid the first two but the third caught him a glancing blow on the shoulder. It felt like he'd been smashed with a club. Which he had.

If he used his knife, people would find the bodies. The police would come. He'd gain precious moments but once they figured out he was a foreigner, they'd give the information to the internal security services. These two had to live.

The kid windmilled the nunchuck in front of him then snapped it forward. Kane threw himself

to one side and came up hard against the wall between urinals. Without thinking he scooped up the
urinal deodorizer block, a bright pink cake the size
and shape of a hockey puck and flipped it at the kid.

The move startled him, and the kid made a little
yelp of dismay and jumped away. Kane used the
moment to free his belt from his pants.

"What's the matter?" Kane asked. "A little piss
never hurt anyone."

"Reaper, bad copy over," Hennessey interrupted.
"Did I copy you urinated on the subjects?"

Kane ignored her. Barely.

He took the belt so the buckle dangled. Holding
the other end, he wrapped it around his wrist then
twice around his palm, leaving about a foot and
change dangling. The thin kid eyed the improvised
weapon. Someone tried to enter the bathroom and
the valet kept them out. He snapped something at
the kid.

Nodding, the thin kid shuffled forward. Kane
took a side stance with his leg leading, keeping the
hand with the belt in the power position. He began
swirling the belt. They eyed each other. The kid
was fast, but he gripped the handle tighter before
he fired an attack and his knuckles stood out white.

Kane leapt forward, darting toward the weak
side. The kid tried to pivot and strike and he was
quick enough that Kane had to block the blow. His
arm exploded with pain, but he'd caught the blow

along the thick knot of his flexor carpi muscles instead of a place where the bones were closer to the surface and he didn't lose the use of it.

He slapped the buckle into the kid's face and his front two teeth cracked. The kid cried out, eyes crossing in pain and Kane took his free hand from where it was already above his head, blocking the nunchucks' blow, and drove the heel of his palm into the thin kid's nose.

The nose mushed like fruit, blood and snot smearing across his gaunt, narrow face. The blow drove into his face and knocked his head back against the wall. The back of the kid's skull smacked into the hard, smooth tiles on the wall with an audible *thunk.*

"How's the golden shower party coming?" Hennessey asked.

Kane ignored her. He imagined this was what being married was like.

The kid dropped like a bag of trash down a chute. Shaking out his arm from the creeping numbness of the nunchucks' strike, Kane turned toward the valet. The guy was on him in a whirlwind of strikes and Kane recognized the style as Krav Maga. He covered up like a boxer in the ring and gave ground. He went two steps back, catching blows on his arm, fired the toe of his leather boot into the valet's shin and instantly fed him a hard right with the leather belt wrapped around his knuckles.

At the flash of pain from the kick the valet dropped his guard momentarily. Kane's blow rolled like a train through his weakened defenses and clipped him on the point of his chin. The man's jaw lurched sideways in a motion never intended by nature. The lyrics to Lead Belly's "Good Night, Irene" flashed through Kane's mind as he watched the man drop.

He keyed his Bluetooth. "Coming out."

"What happened?" Hennessey demanded. "Did you exchange digits with your new bros?"

Kane folded his belt to render it less obvious in his hand and went through the bathroom door, moving fast. He kept his head down and made straight for the front of the hotel lobby.

"In a minute," Kane said. "Just be in front and ready to go."

"Copy that."

Kane crossed the floor, avoiding eye contact but scanning best he could to see if he noticed anyone else observing him. He thought he was safe but couldn't be sure as he was still wired from the sudden jolt of adrenaline. As he stepped out into the heat, Hennessey came to a stop directly in front of him. He got in and she turned to him.

"Tell me you washed your hands."

"Drive," he snapped.

"Oh man, you didn't wash your hands. That's nasty."

"Drive, goddamn it."

Hennessey pulled out into traffic, speed shifted up, taking the RPMs into the red and sped away. Kane leaned back, rubbing his shoulder where the nunchucks had struck him. He'd thought Axe was an aggressive driver; Hennessey appeared suicidal in her vehicle operation.

And she didn't shut up.

"What kind of adult doesn't wash their hands after touching pee? Your mama not teach you to wash your hands after getting piss on them? I mean…"

Kane tuned her out. He was getting better at it.

CHAPTER 6

The safe house was in a quiet neighborhood halfway between Zahedan and the International Airport. It blended in well with the other homes and was nondescript tan stucco. They'd utilized the habit of not getting out of the car until inside the garage with the door down to prevent random interactions with the neighbors.

Kane washed his hands in the kitchen and wished he could have a beer. The country was dry, though legal allowances were made for non-Muslim citizens. In practice, this meant non-Muslims had to brew their own. The safe house wasn't set up for home brewery.

Hennessey sat at the kitchen table and began hooking coaxial cables between a laptop and a PC that had been placed with the house.

"No beer," she said, reading his mind. "But momma doesn't think fighting for freedom should be thirsty work. If you look in the cabinet under the sink, you'll find some Crown Royal."

"Thanks," Kane grunted. He opened the door and grabbed the bottle there.

"I smuggled it in by shoving it up a camel's ass," she said.

Kane froze. He inspected the bottle he was holding.

"Just kidding." Hennessey laughed. "I swiped four bottles out of a consulate bar in Tehran three years ago."

Kane laughed despite himself. There was something about her indefatigable irreverence that was growing on him. She was dysfunctional as hell, which meant she functioned in this world of lies and violence very well. It was a world Kane also felt at home in, as long as he thought the cause was just. He poured himself a generous slug into a glass he got from the cabinet above the stove.

"You mind making that two?" she asked.

"Not a problem," Kane said. "Drinking and intelligence analysis go together like peanut butter and jelly."

"I'm uploading the drive into a secure cloud," she explained. "I'm letting the tech whiz kids on the other side of the satellite do the heavy lifting. They'll crack this encryption and feed me the goodies."

Kane set the glass down in front of her. "Fair enough."

"Here's to finding Naci Sherifi Zindashtia with his pants down and his finger in his butthole."

"Uh, okay." Kane touched his glass to hers. "I'll drink to that."

Hennessey eyed him over the rim of her glass. He felt the weight of her stare and the energy between them suddenly felt different. Not knowing what else to do, Kane sat down in one of the chairs at the table.

Hennessy took a sip. She was still looking at him. He looked back. She smiled. It was more of a smirk.

"I love my job," she said.

"Yeah?"

"And I'm good at it. Which poses a problem."

"Such as?"

"I can't exactly hop on *eHarmony.com* and meet a nice guy when I'm continuously stuck in camel-ass stretches of deserts, hunting jihadists and narco-terrorists."

"No. I guess not."

Hennessy stood up. She was five foot nothing and was still rocking the stick-insect on hunger strike look. That wasn't exactly Kane's type, but she was undeniably attractive. He found himself wondering what that body looked like under her clothes. A xylophone with erogenous zones…

"And you can forget about seeing someone you're stuck on a FOB with."

She stood in front of him. He sat his glass down.

"It'd be career suicide," Kane agreed.

"So, I figure a nice alpha who's only passing through and I won't see again is probably my ideal right now."

Her lips were inches from his. Their breaths mingled and Kane felt himself responding. When she put her hand between his legs, Hennessy felt it too.

"Carpe diem," he said.

"Shut up," she said.

They went at it right where they stood. Then again in the bedroom. After that, Kane had his second drink.

———————

Two hours later a pop up blinked on Hennessy's screen. She was in a tee-shirt, no bra and just her panties. Her red hair was wild. Kane had slid on a pair of jeans but nothing else. He was trying to figure out how to defrost hamburger in the safe house microwave and failing.

"Piece of shit," he said. "You shouldn't have to Google this crap. It should just be a button."

"We got our intel decrypted," she said.

"Fuck it," Kane decided. "We'll eat out."

He walked over to the dining room table and stood behind Hennessey as she opened the files.

"Looks like we've zeroed in on all the naughty," Hennessy said.

"What do you have?"

"The Electronic schematics Naci may have. For the Nuclear centrifuge, and possibly other juicy things according to our in-house nerds."

"Clark was running a counter-intel op and someone's leaving him classified material from *insi*e the place he's trying to defend? I feel that's incongruous."

Hennessey leaned back, looked at him and arched an eyebrow. "Incongruous? How wonderfully well-spoken of you."

"I sense sarcasm."

"You're not completely hopeless then."

"Fifteen minutes ago, I was pretty damn far from hopeless, if I say so myself."

"Touché. But if you think that's incongruous, you're going to love the final bit of skullduggery we acquired."

"What's that?"

Hennessey clicked on an image, zooming in until it filled the screen.

Leaning forward, Kane read the shining tracery of lines and words. Hennessy leaned her head back to rest it against his chest. Her hair smelled like jasmine and oranges from her conditioner. He pushed the scent and the ideas of the things they could do out of his mind. Frowning he read the single line out loud.

"Kathy Dansk is a dupe. What the fuck does *that* mean? Who the fuck is Kathy Dansk?"

"No idea," Hennessey breathed.

"Right?"

"Maybe it's time to go ahead and meet with head of station here."

"Can't do that until morning."

"Really?"

She rose and looked at him, smiling. "Really."

"What ever will we do in the meantime?"

She leaned in close, pressing her braless chest against his and lifting one leg. "I thought all you grunt types wanted to do was workout…"

Kane slid his hands behind her and cupped her buttocks. With ease he picked her up. Giggling, she wrapped her legs around his waist. He felt the grin on his face. It felt big and kind of dopey. He didn't mind.

"Well," he said, "maybe we can start with three or four thousand inverted ab crunches?"

"Thousand?" she mocked.

"It's a start."

CHAPTER 7

Hennessy drove the Audi to station house Iran. Kane rode shotgun and went over files that Hennessey's research elves had provided this morning. It gave him a good feel for the environment, but also raised almost as many questions as it answered.

"Walk me through it," Hennessy said.

"You read it over breakfast," Kane pointed out.

She ran a stop sign, tacked the RPMs into the 5-thousands, and speed shifted through three gears. Kane could hear the tranny screaming for mercy.

"I think better when processing verbally. It's my ADD. Plus, I'm curious to hear what your take is." She took an on-ramp like she was trying to achieve take off in a fighter jet.

"Me, grunt. Pretty lady, smart."

"I'm reevaluating my initial impressions. That should make you happy."

"Having to prove I'm not stupid should make me happy?"

She looked at him, grinning like a high school bully. He sort of wished she wouldn't take her eyes off the road as they'd left 70mph behind them about 20mph ago. He knew she was like a wild dog and showing fear would only cause her to become more aggressive.

"Are you going to cry?"

"Only from relief if we make it without crashing."

Hennessy snapped her eyes back to the road, slammed the heel of her hand into the horn and then cut around a slower moving white Toyota pickup truck. Kane got a look at the driver as they shot past. The man looked old enough to be a grandfather and the alarm on his face was comical. The man looked convinced Hennessy was going to kill them.

You and me both, Kane thought.

Kane opened his screen and perused the summaries. Hennessy had requested further information on Kathy Danske and her place of employment, the Danish Data Institute. It seemed mostly typical background stuff at first glance.

"Dansk, mother Iranian, father an American drilling engineer working for a German oil company."

"Daddy's little princess," Hennessy agreed. "But

then she found Allah."

"I don't understand."

"The mother was an Iranian Christian, the dad while not overtly religious was from Texas, and so, you know, Baptist. Kathy's idea of rebelling was to embrace the Shia faith.

The facility was disguised as an American export business specializing in selling Persian rugs into the US and European markets. Situated in the business district, the building was newer construction and three stories tall.

"Bottom floor is reception in the front and the rest given over to warehouse space," Hennessy explained. "Second floor is the business office and third is extensively dedicated to corporate management."

"But that's where the secret squirrel stuff happens," Kane observed.

"Exactly. There's a Cray supercomputer up there and CIA Tech Division has layered in all kinds of security."

The street was busy, but Hennessy double parked without hesitation. Car horns blared at them in protest as Kane and she got out. The CIA officer flipped them off with casual contempt. Traffic began edging past as they made their way across the sidewalk.

"Not exactly low profile is it?" Kane asked.

Hennessey smiled. "I'm hiding in plain sight.

Old tiger hunter's trick."

"Tiger hunter's trick?"

"Makes sense if you don't think about it," she said. "Now open the door for a lady."

Kane did as requested, and they entered an oasis of soft lighting and sixty-eight degree air conditioned temperature. After the glaring Middle Eastern sun and boisterous cacophony of the city just outside, the effect was disconcerting.

Kane scanned the lobby as they crossed to reception. It was minimalist, modern, and pricey. He was far from an aficionado, but he realized the five-foot ceramic vases were expensive. The same went for the rugs, presumably meant to serve as display models for the company. He noted the unobtrusive black bubble in the ceiling above the door behind the receptionist. He had a hunch that if anything untoward happened there'd be a plethora of unpleasant surprises for any would-be trouble makers.

The woman behind the desk was beautiful, Iranian, conservatively dressed and spoke with a slight British accent.

"Welcome to Krogan Emporiums, how may I be of service?"

Hennessy handed her identification from the car-sized vault in the floor of the safe house. "You can start by reading this and tell your boss his ten-am is here."

The woman's eyes glittered but her smile remained in place. "But of course. Won't you have a seat? I'll just be one moment."

"Tout de suite," Hennessey said. "I don't have time to play with the help."

The smile was gone. "But of course," the receptionist said.

Kane and Hennessey took seats on a divan that looked like the mutated lovechild of Franklin Lloyd Wright and a drunk Ikea designer. It was part bench, part couch, part spaceship, and all uncomfortable.

Must cost a fortune, Kane thought. *Strong use of tax dollars.*

He shoved the palm leaf of a potted rubber plant out of his face. "Little hard on the lady, weren't you?"

Hennessey made a scoffing sound. "I didn't hear any complaints about my personality last night. Either time. Or this morning."

Kane sighed. "You know, there's an old saying. Someone who's nice to you but an asshole to the waiter, is still an asshole."

"You seem fixated on assholes, Kane. You need to get something off your chest? I mean if you want, I can turn over, bite the pillow and lower my voice if it would help..."

"How are you still single?" Kane asked.

The receptionist cleared her throat politely. Hennessey and Kane looked up. "Please go through the door. Deputy Director Kohl will see you. Down the hall, second door to the left."

Kane nodded as they rose. Hennessy wasn't so quick. She fixed the receptionist with a stare. Kane noted that the redhead had just enough wildness to her to appear menacing when she wanted. It was like you couldn't entirely be sure that, decorum or not, laws or not, the wiry woman might not just come unglued and deck someone at the slightest provocation.

The receptionist's expression showed doubt and unease as Hennessy invaded her personal space.

"Kohl?" Hennessy spat. "Why am I meeting with Kohl and not Mundt? You think I don't rate the Director?"

The woman looked around nervously. No one had entered while they waited, so unless Iranian spies were hiding under the furniture, Kane didn't see why they needed to be apprehensive about speaking openly.

"Your issue is a matter of counterintelligence," the receptionist said. "Deputy Director Kohl coordinates those activities at this station. It's his direct area. It was deemed he could most easily assist you."

Kane thought that a reasonable answer. Hennessy snarled like her mother had just been insulted.

"We'll see," she said and walked off at a brisk pace.

Kane looked at the receptionist and shrugged. Usually he played the heavy. It was amusing to see the ballerina-sized hellcat taking the role on. He was growing quite curious to see how her style played out. If he was being honest, he didn't understand it all. It was a fun ride so far, though.

He put his hands in his pockets in a casual manner and followed Hennessy as the receptionist buzzed them behind the interior lobby door. They entered a nondescript hallway. The walls were wood panel, the carpet expensive. The Persian motif from the lobby had been dropped in favor of a hybrid between New York business casual and Government Office.

When the lobby door closed behind them, he could tell the door was solid, blast proof. He was behind the curtain now, where the black magic happened. Hennessy set off down the hallway without looking back. A woman in a modest business skirt, blouse, and hajib came around a corner, reading some files.

She looked up, saw Hennessy charging her and tried to smile a greeting. Half a second later she realized the little ginger had no intention of stopping, and jumped out of her way. The woman hit the wall with her shoulder and pressed the file to her chest.

"Rude much?" the woman snapped.

"You don't know the half of it," Kane said.

Down the corridor Hennessy stopped in front

of a door and Kane stepped up beside her. The CIA officer scowled, eyes narrowing at the closed door. A plaque on the door read Simon Kohl, Executive VP Customer Relations.

"The sonofabitch couldn't be bothered to even step out in the hall to greet us?" she spat.

"Uh—" Kane started.

"*Fine*," Hennessy seethed. "He wants to wave cocks around? Wait until he gets a load of mine."

"As someone who's recently slept with you, I'm not sure how I should take that statement," Kane observed.

"Game face on, Reaper," she said.

Hennessy threw the door open without knocking and went in like a SWAT team serving a warrant. Kane followed her through, closing the door behind him. The office screamed "*monied macho*", dark wood paneling and cabinets, shag carpet, a ridiculously large oak desk as a centerpiece. A liquor service tray with expensive decanters (presumably because having the actual bottle would be gauche) and cut-glass tumblers.

Brass fixtures such as a ship compass and other nautical instruments were scattered around as decor. The place smelled like good whiskey, expensive aftershave, and deception. If there'd been a tiger skin rug on the floor Kane wouldn't have been shocked.

The man he took to be Kohl stood behind the

desk, rising at Hennessy's dynamic entry. The look on his heavy-jowled face was somewhere between shock and outrage. The Deputy Director stood six feet and was running close to three hundred pounds in a tailored power suit of walnut brown. A gold signet ring set on one fat pinkie. A close but thick beard lined his soft jaw, attempting to camouflage a weak chin. Brown eyes, hawk sharp and bright, darted above a Roman nose that betrayed the flush of a pint a day of liquor, minimum, drinker. His thinning hair was greased back and pulled into a Euro-trash ponytail.

When he spoke, his baritone betrayed his indignation.

"What is the meaning of—"

"That's what I want to know," Hennessy interrupted. "You think I'm here to accommodate you? Jesus, what else do you want? A blowjob?" She leaned forward and jammed a finger at Kohl. "Oh, that *is* it, isn't it? I'm a woman so you're going to make me provide sexual favors to get the operational support I need. That's fucking well going in my report."

Kohl made a strangled sound. It seemed like a denial, righteous outrage, and flustered battle cry had knotted up in his throat. His face was strobe light red. A thick vein at his temple bulged. He clenched his hands into fists and knuckles popped like gunshots.

"Get out," he managed to sputter.

"Fuck that," Hennessy snapped. "I'm doing God's work and your pride isn't going to screw up my operation."

"Is this normally how you secure cooperation?" Kane asked. He nodded at Kohl. "Hello, I'm Kane."

"And I'm Cindi fucking Lauper. You want me to sing 'True Colors' with that blowjob?"

With a great effort Kohl settled himself down. His nostrils flared as he slowed his breathing. Hennessy, seemingly happy the man was suitably off center by her entrance wandered over to the service table and poured a splash of whiskey into a glass.

Kane watched Kohl rearrange his expression. He snorted softly and faked a chuckle. He sat back down in his thousand-dollar Concorde office chair. He stepped his blunt fingers and eyed Kane.

"Are you going to be offering me oral sex as well?"

Kane raised his eyebrow. "Not anytime soon."

Kohl nodded. He turned to Hennessy. "You seem agitated. How can we move forward?"

Hennessy tossed back her drink, flicked an ornate porcelain coaster to one side and set the glass down directly on the wood. Kane saw the vein above Kohl's eye throb again, but the man made no comment.

"We need to talk about your missing boy, a little

Persian hottie by the name of Kathy Dansk, and motherfucking Midnight."

Kohl grunted. He smoothed his hair with a slow gesture, wearing the expression of a man trying to solve a difficult Algebra equation. After a moment he looked up at Hennessy then over to Kane.

"Not here," he said. "You have a car?"

"Nope," Hennessy replied. "Flew here on a flying carpet your mom gave us."

Kane bit the inside of his cheek to keep from laughing. He cleared his throat and then nodded.

"What she means is, yes, we do have a vehicle."

"Good. You can follow me. We'll have an early lunch."

"Fine," Kane agreed.

Instead of making a joke about Kohl obviously enjoying too many early lunches, or saying something vulgar and insulting, Hennessy just nodded.

"Sounds good. I'm sure my operational contact was included in your brief. Text us the address and we'll meet you there."

"I'm ever so much looking forward to it," Kohl said, managing to keep his sardonic edge to a minimum.

———

They met Kohl at a hole-in-the-wall Persian restaurant at the edge of the city's main bazaar. It was quiet and cool inside with a softly gurgling fountain as a centerpiece. They sat on rugs and the food was served on low tables. After the waiter took their orders Kohl passed a manila envelope to Hennessy.

"Here," he said.

Hennessy took it and set it beside her without looking inside. "That our support materials?" she asked.

Kohl grunted in the affirmative and then the waiter brought their orders. The man dug in with vigor, completely without self-conscious reflection. Kohl didn't seem to mind talking with his mouth full.

"Corporate ID for the Institute, a change of passports, and two secure phones. You are registered with the police under those passports. Registry is required and if you're stopped without the proper paperwork there'll be problems."

"Goody," Hennessy said. She lit a cigarette. "Uncle Kohl is giving us nice presents."

Kane had checked and double checked as they made the drive but neither he nor Hennessey had been able to detect any surveillance efforts. Now he surreptitiously scanned the restaurant. His experience in the hotel lobby left him guarded and wary.

There were twelve other diners, each tucked into the recesses of partial alcoves. The acoustics were muted and the susurration of the fountain left the clientele able to converse in relative privacy. Short of a directional mike he didn't think they would be overheard.

Kohl waved a fork. "I came to the Middle East as a lieutenant in Army Intelligence back during Gulf One. I stayed deployed in Kuwait until I resigned my commission and joined the agency. They sent me right back here. I've been here ever since. Midnight is the Middle Eastern counterintelligence version of my white whale. I've been chasing her from Lebanon to Yemen and all points between. This isn't the first time she's been linked with international narcotic smugglers. She seems to like their ready-made networks for her operations."

"So, what happened?" Hennessey asked. She lit a cigarette.

"So, Clark crosses her path and doesn't come through me?" Kohl grunted. "That's not a good sign. It bothers the hell out of me, and it should you as well, assuming you're experienced enough to grasp the connotations."

"Why do you think that happened?" Kane asked. He wasn't going to let the man's arrogance goad him.

"He's either dead or gone over," Kohl said immediately. "*Obviously,*" he emphasized the word so hard the implied insult almost dripped off it like syrup.

"It's not that he doesn't trust you?" Hennessy

asked.

Kohl set his fork down and leaned back. He appeared nonplussed by the accusation. He ran his tongue along his teeth then pursed his lips.

"If he doesn't trust me then it's because he's been compromised." He smiled at Hennessy. "Forgive me saying so, but my operations here are not para-military. I'm not hiding out in the ass end of no-where in a war zone. My cover is deep, the chance of exposure high. This sort of thing requires a subtlety I'm not sure you," here he nodded at Kane, "or someone from special operations, are suited for. We are playing a game of nuance here."

Hennessey inhaled on her cigarette, meeting Kohl's eyes. She breathed out and a cloud of gray smoke filled the space between them.

"I may not be the solution you want," she said. "But I'm the solution you have. So, thanks for the lecture on tradecraft, but why don't you give me something I can use?"

Kane watched them. He didn't trust Kohl and he couldn't tell if that was because he disliked him on a personal level so much, or if he was getting true, professional warning vibes from the man. This was Hennessy's AO; he'd let her handle it. Kohl wasn't wrong about one thing though; Team Reaper did not roll subtle, as a general rule.

Kohl smoothed his hair back, plastering the thinning strands to his pate as if trying to iron the wrinkles out of clothing. He worried the signet ring on his pinkie with one thick thumb. His nails were manicured and lightly buffed.

"Kathy Dansk," he said. "Clark was running an investigation or surveillance op that started focusing on her. I can upload her bio on the secure cloud. She might provide a lead for what Clark was doing before he disappeared."

As he talked, Kane finished his food. He saw an old man the approximate age of Methuselah, face deeply seamed, watching them as he lounged next to a hookah. Kane looked away. It didn't seem likely Iranian intelligence was using octogenarians as operatives, but his experience in counter-guerilla operations told him not to dismiss anyone out of hand based solely on their looks.

Hennessy nudged him and stood. Kane followed suit, checking the restaurant once more. Kohl didn't rise with them and no one offered to shake hands. They curtly nodded their goodbyes but just as they were about to leave, Kohl spoke again.

"This is my area of operations," he said, voice gravel and sandpaper. "I expect professional courtesy in that regard. All agency resources come through me and anything *remotely* like Direct Action I expect to know about before it happens, otherwise I'll go right to the head MENA," he said, using the official acronym for the Office of Middle East and North Africa Analysis.

Hennessey gave him a tight smile. "We measuring dicks again? Okay. My operational tasking isn't regional, Kohl, it's transnational. I get my play-in-the-sandbox-papers from the Crime and Narcotics Center. He's rolling under the authority of the Worldwide Drug Initiative. But you'd already know that if you read the brief on me. Since I know you wouldn't overlook background, I assume this must be you trying to bluff me." Her smile was gone. "Don't try and bullshit a bullshitter."

Kane stepped forward. He caught Kohl's eye and held it. "You go ahead and talk to General Thurston at WDI, she'll let you know what you can do if you have a problem with how I run my ops. Or the ensuing body count that frequently occurs. Get in my way and get stepped on."

Not waiting for a reply Kane turned and strode for the door, Hennessey stretching her legs to match his long, quick strides. He held the door for Hennessey and as she went through, he looked back. Kohl was on his phone, face seething with rage.

CHAPTER 8

Kane used a small mirror on an extendable handle to quickly check for bombs. He lifted the hood and ran a practiced eye over the engine compartment. Doing a down and dirty field bomb security check wasn't exactly something you filed under *"low profile"*, but everything felt off about this operation and his well-honed paranoia horn, a must-have item in combat, was ringing like a klaxon.

Popping the locks, he slid behind the wheel while Hennessey climbed in and opened her laptop. He pulled into traffic as she brought her information up.

"Man, there's something about stomping a man's balls into the dirt that gets me hot and bothered," she said.

"You rattled his cage pretty hard," Kane said.

"I did? What about you going all alpha male there at the end?"

"I've had to deal with too many operations officers like that," Kane said. He spoke as if the memory left a literal bad taste in his mouth. "Desk jockeys who figure because they point the shooters where to go that makes 'em top dog. They hide behind their office and their rank and talk a lot of shit to better men."

"I get all weak in the knees when you talk dirty like that," Hennessy replied.

Kane shot her a glance and grunted. After a moment he asked, "Kohl upload the files?"

Hennessey was thumbing her phone screen. "Yes, I've got Kathy Dansk's vitals all right here including cell number and residence. You want to check her out?"

"Tell me you don't trust Kohl," Kane said.

"Depends on what you mean by trust," Hennessy said. She lit a cigarette and cracked the window. "Do I think he'll waste any time trying to be petty and backstabbing me to his superiors? Yes. But do I think he's a traitor? No."

"He likes living the good life."

"Yeah, he does. He must have shit sideways for joy when the home office set his cover up as a successful international merchant. Why? You saying you think he's a rogue information dealer?"

Kane's Spidey-sense was making his knuckles white on the wheel. "I'm saying I don't like him."

"No shit, you don't like him, he's a fat ass who

dresses like a Eurotrash. But he's right about having a lot of years in the Middle East. Rumor has it he had Uday Hussein as an asset and was trying to talk him in when the Delta boys from Task Force Twenty turned him and his brother into dog food. His connections run deep in this region and he's sparred with all the shadow players. He's decided to be too much of an asshole for us to get on his good side now, but my tough talk aside, we may not want to cross him too hard."

Kane nodded. "Fine. Let's put a pin in it and focus on Dansk."

"I got something else you can stick a pin in, Jarhead."

Kane burst out laughing. "It's like I'm in a car with a nineteen year old Marine."

"Shit, my testosterone levels are probably higher."

"I don't know how to respond to that."

"Then shut up and drive where I tell you, save some of that Captain America charm for Kathy Dansk. Of course, she hates westerners, so you know, good luck with that."

CHAPTER 9

Kathy Dansk lived in an upscale apartment building in the center of the city. Whatever her new-found dedication to the cause of global Islamic revolution, it hadn't caused her to forsake the better things in life, Kane reflected.

"Seem like our pious little girl is living beyond her means?" Kane asked.

"She's got money in the family," Hennessy reminded him. "Maybe Mommy and Daddy are underwriting her devoutness."

Kane double parked in front of the building. Traffic fines could come out of Hennessy's operational budget.

"That seem a bit modern for Iran?" he asked.

They got out of the car, ignoring angry honks, and crossed the sidewalk toward the door of the building.

"Yeah," she admitted. "A little bit. Not outside

the realm of possibility, but unusual."

Kane scanned the street as they reached the door. A block down, a young man on a beat-up Honda 250cc motorcycle, pulled the bike out of traffic and up onto the sidewalk. He wasn't wearing a helmet.

A lone male, fighting age. Kane cataloged him automatically. The reflex was born more of rooting out terrorist from among common villagers while serving as a Marine than any espionage tradecraft. The man wore a light tan windbreaker, dark blue jeans and Nike cross trainers.

As Kane watched, the man knelt beside his still running bike and took a screwdriver out. Kane heard the engine rpm tone shift as he adjusted the carburetor.

"Trouble?" Hennessy asked.

Kane turned toward. "Probably not. Let's go."

He pulled open the heavy glass door and Hennessy walked through. Following her through he felt the climate control inside the building lobby cool his skin. There was bright linoleum under his feet, track lighting overhead.

To one side sat a bank of elevators, opposite them a reception desk facing a softly gurgling fountain the size of a Honda Civic. Beyond the fountain were two-story floor-to-ceiling windows set around a massive revolving door like the kind found in airport terminals. The decor was muted, but subtly expensive.

"She's on the fourth floor," Hennessy said. She headed toward the elevators.

"Shouldn't she be at her job?"

"Jesus, Kane, you knuckle-dragger. Didn't you know today is *Eid-e-Fetr?*"

"Gazuntite."

"The end of Ramadan, Jarhead. Public holiday. We have as good a chance catching her at home as anywhere else."

"Our export cover company was open," he pointed out as they reached the elevators.

"Yes, but we're infidels."

He pushed the UP call button. "Good to know."

"I assume you're up for tossing the place top to bottom if the little minx isn't available to an intimate little tête-à-tête?"

"B&E is a hobby of mine," he replied.

There was no answer when Hennessy rang the bell or knocked.

"The little angel does not appear to be in residence," Hennessy noted.

"Let's do this," Kane agreed. "Watch the hall."

He pulled an electric lockpick tool from a pocket and went to work on the door. First, he slipped in a tensioner bar about two and a half inches long. He slipped the pick in then slid it out back from the actuator in the lock. He thumbed the juice, the device vibrated like a hyperactive electric toothbrush as the pins locked in place, and he turned the tension bar like a key, unlocking the door. He repeated the process with the deadbolt above the door handle and they were inside the apartment in under twenty seconds.

As Hennessy entered, Kane checked up and down the hallway a final time. As he did, the elevator dinged and the motorcycle rider from the street stepped out. Putting a hand on Hennessy's back he pushed her inside and closed the door behind him.

She looked back, hand reaching behind her for her pistol. He shook his head and held his finger to his lips. He didn't want them to speak normally until they were sure no one was actually in the apartment. Leaning down he whispered into her ear.

"Someone followed us up from the street. I'm going to deal with them. If you need help, holler and I'll come running."

She nodded once. The pistol came out and she stepped deeper into the apartment. Kane turned and left through the door. Operating on the fly, Kane made several quick decisions. If the man was letting himself into an apartment, he'd let him go. If the man was gone he'd stop pursuit. If the man was still hanging out in the apartment he was going to put him down, non-lethally if possible.

Coming out the door he found himself ten feet from the man. His eyes widened as Kane emerged.

Kane smiled and pointed with his chin, "Hey is that police?"

The man blinked in momentary confusion and Kane struck without hesitation. He executed a smooth shuffle-step, closed the distance, and jammed the ends of his stiffened fingers into the man's throat just below the Adam's apple. The guy gagged and bent at the waist, hands going to his throat on reflex. Kane clinched a bastardized Muay Thai headlock on him and then snapped his knee up into the guy's face several times.

The impacts shuddered through the man's body and he felt the nose explode under his strike. He paused, shifted his feet to change his angle of attack and the man's hand appeared from his jacket pocket. There was a push-button stiletto in his grip. The blade jumped out the end of the handle and the man took a wild slash.

Kane shuffled backward and the point of the knife cut open air. The man used the break to retreat. As he straightened Kane saw his face was a mask of blood where he'd broken the man's nose. The man snarled a curse in Farsi and feigned a fencer's lunge, forcing Kane back a step.

The man feinted an attack step causing Kane to check, then turned and ran. Kane cursed then followed. He had his SIG, but he wasn't ready to gun the man down. Disposing of a body in an apartment building was going to be more complicated than the trouble it was worth. Things might quickly nosedive in that direction, but for now he was keeping this hand-to-hand.

If the guy escaped and called for backup or even just to report suspicious activity to the police, it would cut short their ability to thoroughly search Dansk's home. For better or worse, Kane decided to beat the man into submission.

He sprinted after the man, who passed the elevator banks without a glance and made for the fire stairs door at the end of the hallway. Kane dug deep and put on an extra burst of speed. The man reached the door and spun. Striking out with the blade he forced Kane back long enough for him to slip out of the hall and onto the stairs.

Kane followed, bullying the door open hard in hopes of catching the man if he'd planned on doubling back into an ambush strike. The man was down a flight of stairs and gaining speed. The fire stair was of standard design, the distance between each floor broken by two flights of steps running parallel to each other. The man swung around the railing and plunged down the second half of the stairs. Kane put a strong hand on the metal railing and hopped over just as the man drew even with him.

The former Marine's big feet smashed into the fleeing man's head and shoulders, well over two hundred pounds crashing down. The man folded like cheap lawn furniture and cried out as his legs twisted painfully beneath him and he was driven into the cement steps.

Kane sprawled as he landed and came down draped over the top of the man. His left hand shot down and snatched the man's wrist, immobilizing the knife. The man squirmed and Kane sort of surfed along his flailing body and limbs. When his feet found purchase on the steps Kane took his free hand and shoved two fingers up the man's nostrils, slamming his head back.

Tears immediately leaked from the man's eyes and his struggles slowed. His free hand tried to punch at Kane, but it was an easy matter for the former Marine to stifle the blows with his elbow. Quickly the man was reduced to ineffectually pawing at Kane as he writhed in pain.

"That's it," Kane urged him. "Drop the knife and we can talk about how I might have been a trifle rude during our getting-to-know-each-other period."

The man glared in response. Kane bore down on the trapped wrist and finally the man dropped it. It clattered loudly as it tumbled down the stairs. Above them the hydraulic hinge on the door breathed and footsteps descended the steps. Kane tensed and the man rolled his eyes upwards hopefully.

Hennessy appeared at the top of the steps. Her pistol was out.

"Making new friends?" she asked.

"You try talking to him," Kane suggested. "He's been extremely recalcitrant in our conversation."

"You sure the little dear speaks English?"

"For his sake I hope so." Kane smiled down at the man. "Because otherwise he isn't going to understand why he's being put in so much pain."

Kane straightened his arm, pushing his two fingers deeper into the man's tender nasal cavities. The man cried out in pain, eyes scrunching up as more involuntary tears poured from his eyes.

"You're hurting his feelings," Hennessy said.

"I don't like being followed," Kane replied.

Hennessy sighed and spoke in rapid-fire Farsi. Slowly Kane felt the man relax under his grip.

"What do you want?" His English was heavily accented but quite understandable.

"First thing I want," Kane told him, "is for me to stop having to lay on top of you like this is a date. I'm getting up; you move and she shoots you, understand?"

The man scowled, then nodded. Kane rose and expertly frisked him. He had a couple of hundred dollars' worth of Iranian rials in his pocket but no wallet or ID. Kane took a burner cell off him. He didn't have another weapon Kane could find. Kane used one foot to skid the knife across the floor to the opposite side of the landing.

"You stay right there."

"You already have my money," he protested. "Just take it and leave me alone."

"Oh, well played," Hennessy scoffed. "Yes, you're just an innocent bystander we're trying to rob."

"What else would I be?"

"Guidance police checking on westerners," Hennessy said. "Or you could keep an eye on us for money. But if you keep claiming innocence, my friend is going to pick your nose again."

Instinctively the man's hand went to his face. He didn't seem eager to repeat the experience.

"Let me go," he said. "I wasn't supposed to interact with you, just report what you did."

"To who?" Kane demanded.

"I don't know," he said. "I'm not with the police. I just sometimes run errands."

"What neighborhood you from?" Hennessy asked. "Where in the city?"

"Shirabad," he said.

Hennessy grunted. "Give him back his money," she told Kane. "He can go."

Kane lifted an eyebrow, the CIA officer nodded once. "Path of least resistance. But you leave the knife with us."

"Whatever," the man agreed, voice sullen. He rose to his feet, expression a humorous mixture of petulant and wary.

Kane smiled very big. It didn't seem to reduce the man's tension. "By all means scoot along, you scamp," Hennessy said. "Neither one of us has the slightest interest in trying to dispose of a body."

The man made up his mind and quickly moved down the stairs, looking back over his shoulder as he went. Kane tried smiling nicely again. The man fled more quickly and soon they heard him several flights down before he took a doorway.

"Why cut this short," Kane asked, "other than the fact exposure is a constant issue?"

"He's either not a pro, or such a pro that he can fool me into thinking he's not a pro. If that's the case, then he's probably too good to break quickly. If he's a disposable cutout then he likely has shit to tell us." She indicated the stiletto. "Take the knife. We'll upload his prints. *That*'ll probably tell us more. Besides, I want to finish tossing Dansk's apartment and two works faster than one."

"You're calling an audible," Kane said.

"I'm calling an audible," she agreed.

"Except I'm the quarterback. It's up to the quarterback to call the audible on the team."

She slapped his face gently. "Baby, if you have to tell people you're the quarterback, then you're probably not…"

"Maybe we could just toss the apartment?"

"Whatever you say," she smiled. "Just don't forget the knife."

They jogged back up the stairs and headed down the hallway a second time. Each of them was conscious of a ticking clock hanging above their heads. They made the door, double checked and then went in.

They went through the place top to bottom. The interior was as stylish as the high-end address implied. Just inside the door Dansk had an expensive end table of Damascus wood legs and a beaten brass top on which a crystal vase held tulips in several different colors. There was a mirror on one wall and a copper bas-relief of a peasant girl pouring water into a tub. The floor was a green marble tile underfoot.

"Très fashionable," Hennessy murmured.

The short hallway opened up, revealing an archway into a kitchen on the left and living room on the right. Kane looked around, grunted.

"She likes her knick-knacks," he said.

It was true. The soft beige walls contained box shelving like picture frames in asymmetric rows. On them was every sort of curio ornament from small statues in semi-precious metals, clocks, figurines and glassware. These were offset by several paintings, mostly soft watercolors of flowers. There was a fireplace against one wall and on the mantel were more bagatelle items, small sculptures of rearing horses and ancient Persian warriors only several inches high.

One table held a traditional samovar tea kettle, which was usually in use all day long. Kane rested the back of his hand briefly next to the metal. He caught Hennessy's eyes.

"Stone cold," he said.

She nodded—*Good.*

They moved through the apartment, across the open floor design kitchen and into a short alcove holding the door to her bedroom. They worked methodically for several minutes, carefully replacing each item to its exact position. Finally, Hennessy called out from the bedroom.

"Bingo," she said. "Whatever else she might have going on, these should give us the leverage we need."

Kane walked in. "What do you have?"

"I've got diagnostic printouts of several guidance systems the Institute is working on. Someone has been a very naughty girl, only not in any sort of a fun way."

Kane chuckled as he turned to walk toward her voice. At that moment the deadbolt on the door turned over with a heavy metallic *clunk*. He heard keys trying to find the slot in the door handle and he immediately darted over behind the wall to the living area that was next to opening to the entrance hall.

"Company," he hissed.

"Got it," she answered in a whisper.

For one long moment the only sound was the key turning. Then the lock opened, and the door swung open. Footsteps sounded clearly on the floor. Kane eased out a soft breath, ready to spring. The person shut the door behind them and walked down the hall. There was a flash of color and motion as whoever had entered emerged into the living area.

Kane unfolded smoothly. He immediately recognized Kathy Dansk from her picture even as he moved. The woman who opened the door was easily recognizable from the photos in her background file. She was perhaps 5'6" and gently pear shaped, she had an open, attractive face framed by a hijab and wore loose, traditional skirts. Her eyes were very dark brown. He wrapped her up with one arm around her body, trapping her arms to her side. His other hand came down over her mouth, pressing hard to keep her from biting. He lifted.

Dansk squawked as he caught her, but he was able to stifle the sound. She struggled, thrashing in his grip but he had her off the ground now and whatever else she might have been accomplished at, her reactions indicated she hadn't been recruited for her high level of hand-to-hand skills.

"Easy," he said. "I don't want to hurt you, but you need to calm down."

Strangely, this assurance didn't seem to pacify Dansk overmuch and she struggled even harder in his grip. In front of them Hennessy strolled out of the bedroom with a manila envelope in one hand. She leaned casually against the door jamb and began pulling glossy 8x10 photographs out. She made a *tsking* sound like a mother looking at the messy playroom of a young child.

"Someone didn't take her Non-Disclosure Agreement very seriously."

Dansk ceased struggling. Kane gently lowered her to her feet but kept her locked up. When he spoke, he kept his voice calm, like a man talking down a spooked horse. It might be unpleasant, but it was going to be necessary for him to play the thug in this encounter. He didn't like it. He didn't have to like it, he just had to do his job.

"I'm going to release you," he said. "We're going to have a civilized conversation and then my associate and I will leave, and you can enjoy your holiday."

Hennessy smiled. "Exactly how much you're able to enjoy it is yet to be determined and depends heavily on your actions in the next few moments."

"Do we have an understanding?" Kane asked.

After a moment, Dansk nodded. Slowly, Kane released her. When she didn't cry out or try to run, he stepped back. She studied the two Americans with not unreasonable suspicion.

"What do you want?" she asked, her English textbook precise.

Hennessy walked forward, giving the woman little choice but to give way or get run over.

"I guess the first thing I want would be to demand to know why you have sensitive schematics in your personal residence, but since we already know you think you're working for Iranian intelligence, I'm not going to bother."

Kane looked at the woman. She was nervous and trying to hide it. He didn't blame her. Dansk was an asset, not an operative. He took a big breath and let it out slowly. He was getting tired of these seemingly endless rounds of investigation. It was time to put this thing into high gear.

"Where's Clark?" he asked.

Dansk looked like she'd been electrocuted. Her mouth fell open and her eyes widened in surprise reflex as her cheeks colored red. She couldn't have been more obvious with a neon sign flashing *guilty* on her forehead. Swallowing, she tried to compose herself.

"I don't know—"

"Save it," Kane cut her off. "We know you're working for Iranian intelligence. Frankly, I don't give a shit, except that I need Clark. Give us Clark and we go away."

"I think you'd better leave—" she tried again.

This time Hennessy cut her off.

"You know that's not going to happen so shut the hell up with that noise. You are in this situation. You put yourself here with your decisions. Now you need to make some decisions that are going to get you out of it. Where's Clark?"

"If I tell you will you go?" she asked.

"We will," Hennessy nodded. "But I can't promise we won't be back if you lie to us."

There was a long moment and then she seemed to wilt. She nodded once, then again, as if convincing herself.

"Alright," she said. "I'll tell you what I know. It's not much but it should help."

"Do share," Hennessy said.

"As far as I know, based on my last contact with my handler," Dansk said, "he's operating out of a hotel in Zahedan. I don't know why."

Hennessey studied her for a moment. "Give me the address," she said. Dansk did and the CIA officer memorized it after hearing it only once and consisting of names in Farsi. Hennessy held up the schematics.

"I don't know why you had these printed out," she said. "But I'm keeping them. Kudos to you for keeping the laptop I know you must have hidden so well."

Dansk didn't say anything, and Kane stepped forward, towering over the woman. He spoke slowly, locking eyes with her and pinning the woman with his stare.

"In a perfect world," he said, "you'll never see us again. Don't make me come back here."

Dansk looked away, hugging herself. She nodded. Taking that as a good exit point, Kane and

Hennessy left the apartment, moving fast.

"She didn't have a cell phone either," he said. "That seem weird to you?"

"Sure does."

"How likely do you think it is the address will pan out?" he asked.

"I give it as high as fifty-fifty. If it were only one percent we'd still have to check it out at this point. I feel the trail getting colder every minute."

Kane nodded. This Black Swan had a lot to answer for.

CHAPTER 10

"Zahedan is associated with opium smuggling, kidnappings, and religious tensions," Hennessy told him. "It's in a Shirabad neighborhood. Think if ISIS were running 1990's Compton crack trade."

"I don't see us blending in," Kane said. "Even if we could pass for authentic Iranians we'd still be from the wrong neighborhood. We're going to stick out."

Hennessy nodded. "Yeah, we can try and ghost but if we're forced to talk to someone there could be a confrontation."

"Pistols going to be enough?" he asked.

"I'd feel better if you were packing something more substantial. And we're going full body armor, I think."

Kane nodded. "High profile it is."

"And Kane?" Hennessy asked. He looked over and she rested one hand over his.

"Yes?"

"Just remember if you let them get me, then all this sweet birthday cake is gone."

"I'll endeavor to protect my, uh, birthday cake."

"Good boy."

The drive across the city was slow. Traffic was a gridlock mess that Hennessy managed to navigate by operating with suicidal aggression. Things like stop lights and speed signs or turn blinkers all seemed very much optional. Not the horn, the horn was required and from start to finish the drive was a cacophony of blaring car horns in hazes of noxious fumes.

Urban poverty had a look that transcended international borders, Kane decided. The steel and glass of the downtown gave way to blocks of rundown one-story buildings and empty dirt lots. Everywhere, clothing hung out on lines to dry and trash lay uncollected in alleys and along the curbs.

Young men with hostile eyes watched traffic and soon he began noticing steadily increasing graffiti, even if he couldn't read it. Groups of kids chased ancient, peeling soccer balls between corrugated-steel buildings, and everyone smoked. Twice they passed two places roped off by yellow police tape. They crawled through bumper-to-bumper traffic before turning off the main street. The address given them by Dansk turned out to be only on the very fringes of something that could be termed *hotel*. Bail Hostel with its teeth kicked out was more an appropriate description. Hennessy circled the block, giving them opportunity to inspect it from all sides as much as possible.

During the recon cruise they spotted an anonymous alley they thought would work for a staging area. Hennessy pulled in and killed the engine. Together they opened the trunk and began prepping. They snugged vests into place and checked the loads on their PC-9 pistols.

Hennessy pointed at a compact metal briefcase. "Don't say momma never got you anything."

Curious, Kane pulled the case to himself and opened it up. He whistled in surprise. Inside along with two extra stick magazines, was an Uzi Pro. An improved variation on the Micro Uzi, the little chatterbox was just under twenty-one inches long and hardly more than five pounds in weight. A GEMTECH silencer sat in the cut foam next to the machine pistol.

"That's it," he said. "I'm taking you to meet mother."

"I'm not the kind you bring home to meet the parents." Hennessy laughed. Her face grew pensive for a moment. "Never have been," she added in a softer voice.

Kane looked up at the change in tone. He thought he'd heard something there but now her face was a business-like mask as she scanned the alley. He thought about acknowledging what he'd heard, immediately realized she wouldn't appreciate it, and quickly attached the sound suppressor.

Despite the heat he shrugged on a light windbreaker and tucked the Uzi away. "Let's do it," he said.

Hennessy slammed the trunk closed and they went. Rounding a corner they stepped out of the alley and strode up the sidewalk to the cracked asphalt of the parking lot. Crossing it they went through a battered wood door and entered the office.

Hennessy talked to a bored looking teenage boy sitting at the reception counter behind thick safety glass. An old man sat in a hard-plastic chair next to the glassed-in desk and smoked foul-smelling home rolled cigarettes. A radio behind the kid played Sasanian music.

Hennessey rapped the glass and said something in rapid-fire Farsi. The kid scowled and she slid a little wad of rials across the decidedly unsanitary looking counter. The kid took the money, looking mollified and then answered her. Hennessy nodded.

"Let's go," she said.

Kane squinted as they stepped back into the sunlight. He tensed until his eyes adjusted and scanned the parking lot in front of the units. Relentless desert sun had baked the sidewalk brittle.

Brightly colored wrappers littered the ground like confetti. An ancient looking white Subaru was up on blocks across from them, the asphalt beneath it stained in splotches from leaking oil.

A dog nosed garbage under the staircase to the second level. A curtain in one of the windows fell closed as Kane scanned in that direction. Way off in the city a police siren blared into life. He felt like he always did when taking a stroll through Helmand Province, namely that death of some sort was always right around the corner.

He missed his Reaper team. Be that as it may, he still had a job to do.

"Bottom level," Hennessy said. "Last unit."

"Got it," he replied.

They set off toward the rental unit sweating freely in their body armor. Just outside the room there was a mound of cigarette butts, the windows grimy, and paint peeling into splinters on the door jam. Kane frowned at their exposure. He felt like an orphan in a fairy tale who'd followed a trail of breadcrumbs only to end up at the monster's lair.

Find Clark, he thought, *find Midnight. Midnight leads you to Black Swan. Tag Black Swan and go home.* It was simple, direct. It was also the only plan they had. Reaching inside his jacket he gripped the Uzi Pro and nodded at Hennessy.

The CIA officer reached behind her to the small of her back and slid her own hand around the butt of her PC-9. With her other she knocked sharply on the door. There was a long moment then Kane heard someone moving beyond the door.

"We're here for Clark," Hennessy said.

She didn't speak Farsi. If Clark was in there, either he or the people he was with would speak English. There was another pregnant pause then a rough male voice answered in an Iranian accent.

"Does Clark know you?"

"No," Hennessy said. "But we're from his home office and we have the proper bona fides."

There was no answer, but after a moment they heard locks being snapped back and the door swung open. Kane tensed but a man stood in the doorway, hands visible and empty. He was average height, dressed nondescript and had dark stubble covering his face. His eyes were a cold liquid brown the color of weak coffee. They shifted back and forth between them, sizing them up.

"Come in," he said after a moment. "The Ministry has eyes everywhere."

Kane assumed he meant the Iranian Ministry of Intelligence. It didn't seem like something a drug smuggler would worry about it. He still wasn't in a hurry to enter the gloomy room. Hennessy didn't budge, her hand remained on her pistol.

Meeting dangerous people doing dangerous things in dangerous places was her job. Yet every second that ticked forward, measured in heartbeats, Kane's instincts screamed that the situation was edging ever closer to the home turf of a combat marine.

"You know," he said. "You seem like an asshole."

The man blinked in surprise then his face grew red with anger. Kane was already in motion, reaching into his coat he grasped the handle of the Uzi Pro and pulled it clear. His knee came up at the same time, drawn up tight to his chest, and then exploded outward. The heel slammed into the Iranian's gut and drove deep.

Breath spilled from the man's lungs and he folded like bad origami even as Hennessy spun away, drawing her pistol. The man staggered backward, his stumble carrying him back past the partition wall separating the living area from the kitchen.

Someone in the kitchen shouted something in Farsi. Hennessy threw herself down eyes wide with adrenaline. Instinctively Kane jerked to one side and suddenly an avalanche of lead poured through the cheap drywall. Plaster dust exploded in the air and rounds whipped through the living area at waist height. Inside the kitchen the sounds of a suppressed submachine echoed in the confined space.

The man Kane had kicked returned the favor. Rolling up onto one hip he lashed out with his top foot and drove the toe of his shoe into Kane's thigh. Kane grunted under the impact and, already off balance, toppled backward, his ass striking the thin carpet on the floor hard enough to snap his mouth closed. The man dug behind his back for what Kane could only assume was a weapon. Another prolonged burst of automatic fire carved out baseball sized chunks of wall. From his position Kane could just see into part of the kitchen.

"Suppress!" Hennessy screamed.

The PC-9 in her hand went off, unbaffled it sounded like a howitzer in the apartment. Several 9mm rounds punched into the face of the Iranian next to Kane and a blood halo misted as they slammed out the back of his head.

Kane lifted the Uzi Pro in two hands and pulled the trigger. The little blabbermouth came alive in his hands, bucking like a horse as he raked the weapon back and forth. His rounds poured on through the perforated wall, gouging out chunks of the crumbling, collapsing structure in hammer blow impacts.

He was shouting, ears ringing as he swept the muzzle back and forth in a loose z-pattern. Caught in the kill box of an ambush the physics of momentum kept the victims trapped. The only way to break the deadlock was to produce even more violence of action streaming outwards than was being directed inward.

Kane kept the trigger down, firing from his back. He took the Uzi Pro in a one-handed grip and let the weapon kick and buck as he dug for his second magazine. Greasy brass shell casing tumbled out and rattled across the filthy floor. Hennessy belly-crawled past him, heading toward the entry-way to the kitchen.

The Uzi's bolt locked open and he used his thumb to eject the spent magazine.

"Reload!" he barked automatically.

As the spent magazine dropped, Hennessy opened up around the corner, doing an ungainly version of *cutting the pie* corner clearing from the prone.

He slid the full magazine home and felt it *click* into place with the gleeful satisfaction of a kid snapping Lego blocks together. His thumb tapped the release and the bolt slammed home seating the round. He squeezed the trigger, back to his two-handed grip.

Fire no longer came from the far side of the wall and he crunched himself upwards in a sit up, firing tight 3-round bursts of reconnaissance fire. He made it to one knee and paused. Hennessy was on her feet and in a crouch, she swung around the corner at waist level, weapon tracking in front of her. A burst of automatic fire erupted and the CIA officer staggered back.

Kane sprang up and bounded past her. He was on automatic pilot now, his body performing actions without direction. He fired a tight burst through the wall then shuffle-stepped forward and thrust the muzzle around the angle, unleashing everything in blind covering fire. Shielded behind the stream of 9mm Parabellum rounds he snapped his head around the corner after his arm.

Two men were down on the kitchen floor, bleeding out. A third shuddered, his MP5 firing into an ancient stove, as five or eight rounds pounded his chest. Kane let the muzzle climb with recoil, walking a line of slugs up the shooter's sternum and knocking his jaw loose from his face before two slugs cracked the back of his skull open.

Suddenly there was silence.

Breathing hard, Kane forced himself to relax. He checked the bodies, saw only corpses. Turning to Hennessy he found the red head already trying to rise to her feet. He jumped to help her.

"Winner, winner, chicken dinner," she said. Her face was a twisted grimace of pain.

"Your vest catch everything?" he asked.

He ran one hand across her back to check for blood even as he kept the Uzi ready in the other and an eye on the door. She didn't appear to be bleeding. She was leaning against him, obviously fighting through pain. She wasn't a large woman and the kinetic impact of even subsonic rounds at that range would be enough to crack ribs or cause internal concussive damage.

"Think so."

"We've got to get you out of here," he said.

"We need to toss the room," she said.

Kane shook his head. "You're rattled," he told

her. "This was a set up balls to bone. These guys probably don't even have tags in their clothes. We need to scoot."

"The guy who answered the door had a phone," she pointed out. "Get that and we'll call it good."

Kane reached down and grabbed the shirt of the man who'd opened the door. He grunted and yanked him to one side. Brains and bits of skull bone lay on the carpet like chunky soup from where Hennessy had blown his head apart. He saw the blood-smeared phone.

Picking it up he wiped it off on the guy's jeans and put it away. Hennessey stood over by the door, peering out through in an inch-wide crack.

"We good?" he asked.

"We are," she said. "Far as I can see."

"Then let's hustle."

They came out of the room, weapons accessible but low profile. They moved quickly without running. They turned to the hole in the fence they'd noted earlier. People watched them from behind the curtains in the rental units, but no one came outside or challenged them openly.

"They must assume it was rival drug gangs," Hennessy noted.

"Works in our favor," he agreed.

They made it to the car and then drove away calmly. At no point did they hear sirens or pass a police vehicle.

CHAPTER 11

"Dansk set us up." Kane said, cutting the car through traffic.

Hennessy lit a cigarette. "Obviously, but they didn't have a crew of hitters sitting in a rental just waiting for us on the off chance we'd brace her for information."

"Also obvious," Kane agreed. "You think those boys have anything to do with the guy we flushed pulling surveillance on us outside of her apartment to begin with?"

"I don't like coincidences," she released twin jets of blue smoke through her nose in a sigh. "If we go with they're related, then we got one enemy. They're not together? That means multiple groups of hostiles trying to shut us down."

"She sends us to get killed," Kane said, "and then waits for word. We grease those bastards so no one is calling her with the good news. What does she think? What does she do?"

"Boogies the fuck out of there," she said.

"But if Dansk isn't the one calling the shots, then she might not expect to know the outcome."

"I'm not going to accept dead ends," she told him.

"We find a dead end we smash on through," he agreed.

"So Dansk gets a chance to explain herself ?" she said.

"Oh yeah," Kane growled. "The big bad wolf is about to pay Little Red Riding Hood a visit."

They returned to the safe house. They performed first aid, both of them were sheathed in bruises. Despite the discomfort they showered together and made love. The release of adrenaline in the act made it short but intensely powerful. Afterwards they spread analgesic cream across each other's bruises and suited up.

"What time do we go back?" Hennessey asked.

"We don't, I do," Kane replied. He concentrated on lacing up his boots.

"Fuck that."

"No," Kane said. "It needs to work this way."

"Because I don't have a dick?"

"No." He stood up and looked at her. "I have women on my team. You saw Cara; she'll kick anyone's ass, drop the hammer on whoever needs it without her pulse rising."

"Then what?"

"We can't roll without overwatch anymore," he said. "We knew going in that rental could be a trap and we handled it. You did your part. But when it was time to exfil? We got lucky. I need someone to be my eyes and ears when I go in. There are unfriendly operatives crawling all over this thing. We're looking for a ruthless drug lord, and ended up with dysfunction junction crew as our back up. I don't feel good about any of them. We need to go rogue."

Hennessy studied him for a moment. Finally, she got up and went to the fridge. She returned with two bottles of beer.

"Be a fucking gentleman and open my beer, knuckle-dragger."

Kane grinned. He opened the beers while she opened a bottle of Ibuprofen. They drank and it tasted good going down. They took 800mg of the pain reliever. Back in the Corps they'd called Ibuprofen 'Recon candy'. Apparently in the Army it was called 'Ranger Skittles'. Whatever it was called, Ibuprofen was essential to life as an operator.

Hennessy looked at the bottle in her hands, lips pursed.

"There's surveillance gear and two Raven drones in a vault safe under the racks in the garage," she said. "We can wrap you up right," she said.

Kane smiled. "Good."

"Let's go pay our little chick-a-dee a visit, shall we?"

They clinked bottles.

The car rolled to a stop in the alley and Kane got out. Hennessy drove away as he walked to a side door. It was late, deep in the night, past one a.m. The city remained a blaze of light but here in the alley shadows lay thick.

"Comm check," Hennessy said into Kane's earjack.

"Good copy, over," Kane breathed into his mike.

The device nestled against his jaw at the curve of the mandible and broadcast his words by deciphering the vibrations through the bone. It allowed him to speak very softly. He looked back and forth up and down the alley, saw nothing. There were two cameras set on the building. Their earlier reconnaissance had pinpointed this equipment. As a countermeasure Kane wore a black ball cap with IR LEDs in the bill. Naked to the visible eye, the infra-red spectrum light nevertheless blotted the camera optics into smears of bright white light.

As he moved in and out of range of the cameras, he would be covered by what would appear to be intermittent glitches in the video feed. If a living person noticed the malfunction it would be attributed to systemic problems, not individual locations, and thus trigger a diagnostic check, but not a physical response to any one location.

"Go ahead with the jam," he said.

"Copy."

From her car only a block away, Hennessy engaged the next generation radio frequency jammer. The building was not a government facility and its alarm system was commercial. Commercial alarm systems relied on radio frequency to transfer breach data. The jammer, operating in succinct bursts, prevented that.

"You're clear, Reaper," Hennessy said in his ear.

"Making entry."

He quickly inserted the lockpick gun into the keyhole, cranked the lever and heard the brute force attack snap the pins into position. The deadbolt shot back with a greasy, metallic click and the door came open. He ghosted through into the building.

Finding the fire stairs almost immediately, he began climbing. He reached Dansk's floor without incident and slipped into the hallway. Everything was silent, the lighting muted. He waited for a moment, getting a sense of the environment.

"I'm about to make entry," he vibed into the bone mike.

"Copy," Hennessy replied. "I've got zero chatter on cellular networks in the building and the police frequencies display zero alerts to this location."

He strolled down the hall, not moving fast, until he made it to Dansk's door. He stopped, nerves suddenly on fire with a sense of danger. The door stood open two inches. Kane looked sharply left and then right, hand going to his pistol. He still saw nothing. This meant little. Modern flexible optics would allow opposition elements to survey his actions from safely behind the doors of the neighboring apartments.

"Fuck it," he muttered.

"Say again?" Hennessey immediately responded.

"Nothing," Kane said. "That was my inside my head voice."

"Maybe keep it in your head then?" she offered.

Kane didn't reply. He pulled the PC-9 clear and grabbed the doorknob. Lifting to ease the stress on the hinges and reduce any potential squeak, he entered the apartment. Stepping into the narrow hall he went to a knee, pistol up in case of sudden ambush.

Nothing moved. There was no sound. Weapon ready, he gently closed the door behind him. More silence. More stillness. He engaged the deadbolt. If anyone tried to enter after him, he'd have a better chance of detecting them. As for being now locked in with anyone who might already be here, well, it was truer to say they were locked in with *him*.

Edging forward, Kane stepped carefully, giving his eyes time to adjust to the ambient levels of light inside the gloomy apartment. The floor settled softly under his weight as he eased out of the entry and into the living room after clearing the kitchen.

Everything was the same as from his earlier visit. Across the space the door to Kathy Dansk's bedroom stood open.

He shifted his motion into a short, heel-toe shuffle with the pistol's muzzle leading the way. He came up to the jamb and leaned against the wall for several seconds, straining his ears for the slightest sound. Nothing.

He took a snap look.

Kathy Dansk lay face down on the bed, unmoving. Moonlight streamed into the darkened room through windows, leaving pools of inky shadows in the corners. The door to what Kane knew was the master bathroom stood open beyond the bed.

He pulled himself back, waiting to see if his sneak peek triggered a response. When there was none, he changed levels by crouching and entered the room. He crossed the danger zone of the entry fast, moving at a hard angle. Once inside he pivoted smoothly, slamming his butt into a dresser to ensure his back was anchored to a secure location, and then swung the PC-9 around, clearing vectors.

Dansk didn't move.

Kane had seen death before, innumerable times. He knew the unnatural stillness of it. He realized she was dead before he saw where the jet-black pools of her blood had made a soggy mess of her sheets beneath her sliced throat.

Face grim, he edged around the bed and cleared

the bathroom. It was empty. Whoever had sliced Dansk open like Christmas ham was gone.

"Found her," he said into his mic. "She's been killed."

Hennessy responded immediately. "I've got sudden chatter and activity; they're pinging off all around you."

Kane knew The CIA was operating both Bastille corporation Mousejack and Keysniffer in her electronic overwatch. Operating in the 60MHz to 6GHz range she could effectively map all cellular communication devices in a certain area. Those devices would superimpose over existing mapping software to triangulate exact positioning. Once mapped those devices could be monitored for in-going and outgoing signals.

"I've got numerous hits on devices suddenly communicating with each other," she went on. "There's movement all over the imagery. Someone's on to you and they're coming now."

"Copy," Kane said.

He turned and head for the door, moving fast. He snapped back the lock on the front door and checked the hallway.

"You've got a squad sized element moving on the floor above you. At least three more are coming up in the main elevators; hustle, Reaper."

Hennessy's voice remained calm, matter-of-fact; but tension ran in vivid veins through her tone. She was scared, Kane realized. It was not a reassuring epiphany.

Kane entered the hallway. He held the PC-9 up beside his face, muzzle toward the ceiling. He moved with his left hand out a little. Picking up his foot he stepped forward and gently laid it down. He was in a bad way here and knew it. The Iranians were around him on all sides and he wouldn't be making any hasty escapes.

If he wanted out it was going to need to be methodically. Inch forward, listen intently, inch forward more. Sooner or later he'd need to fire, and the decision would happen in heart beats. First the stretched out tension of the sneak and stalk, then a rush of motion and weapon fire. Then he'd either have put a body on the floor or be dead himself.

Toe-heel. Toe-heel. Always keeping his center of balance. Lowering the weapon, he took it in a two-handed grip. Wherever his eyes tracked, so did the barrel. On one side of him ran the railing to the stairwell. He heard the stealthy movement of men below him. Above him floorboards creaked, and he figured at least two more were above him.

His only warning was the rattle of a door handle. In the gloom he'd missed the doorway at the bottom of this flight of stairs. It came open just as he stepped onto the landing. He saw a silhouette, tall and broad. A male. The man held something up in both hands. Act or die.

Kane swung toward, tracking the muzzle of his pistol until it was six inches from the man's face. He closed his non-dominant eye to spare it from the muzzle flash and squeezed the trigger several times. The stairwell lit up like dark clouds in a lightning storm, muzzle flash strobe-lighting in the confined space.

The weapon recoil jumped the handgun in his grip and the flat, hard cracks of 9mm discharges echoed wildly. The figure fell back and hot, sticky fluid splashed Kane's face. The man went down and something metal clattered on the cement floor.

Kane shuffled forward, putting two more fail-safe rounds into the target's head before stepping through the door and putting his back against a wall. He snapped the gun around, covering his vectors of fire. A gunman came around the corner, eyes wide, AKM with paratrooper folding stock in his hands. Kane shot him twice. Blood and brains splashed the wall. The figure slumped to the ground and lay unmoving in a growing pool of red.

Kane spun and sprinted back toward the floor of the landing. He threw his back against the wall and pushed open the heavy door. As it swung back shut, he cleared his angle quickly. It was not a perfect sweep; time was of the essence.

He came through the door, entering the con-crete echo chamber of the stairwell. Excited voices above him, the sound of heavy footsteps on the steps. Crossing the landing he headed down the stairs toward the ground floor. Muzzle first he checked the corner, cleared the threat and then plunged downwards again.

Above him men shouted. A Kalashnikov roared in a heavy metal cacophony. A cyclone of 7.62mm WARSAW rounds ripped into the stairwell. Bullets ricocheted wildly, gouging out splinters of concrete and bouncing uncontrollably. Kane turned another corner and came up to a door. Pistol up and tucked in close to his body he yanked it open.

A tall, gaunt man in the black turban of a Shia clergyman claiming direct descent from Muhammad appeared before. The man's eyes bulged in surprise and terror. Kane didn't notice, his eyes were on the man's centerline and his hands.

Hands told the story in the Shoot/Don't Shoot binary decision tree. Hands with a weapon equated death dealing. Empty hands provoked a second rapid evaluation. The man's hands held a PC-9, the sidearm of the Revolutionary Guard, identical to Kane's.

Kane's weapon discharged from its high tucked position, recoil racking the slide and chambering a second round as a smoking brass casing flew out of the ejection port. The Iranian's face metamorphosed into a gory red rose blossom of blood. Kane stepped over the body, returning to a modified Weaver stance as he moved deeper into this level of the building.

He forced his breathing to slow down, to manage the adrenaline pounding in his body, causing his heart to pound. He felt the euphoric pull of it, fueling his anger, tempting him to cut loose in a firestorm of bullets and death.

He was on the ground floor. It was the front lobby of the building. There was a linoleum floor under his feet, track lighting overhead. To one side sat a bank of elevators, opposite them a reception desk obviously staffed only during business hours. The desk faced a softly gurgling fountain the size of a Honda Civic. Beyond the fountain were two-story floor-to-ceiling windows set around a massive revolving door like the kind found in airport terminals.

As Kane moved forward a police car skidded to a stop just outside. It was a white sedan with a green strip running down the side. Not just police, but Ministry of Intelligence and Security, MOIS, uniformed division law enforcement.

There was no siren, but the lights revolved on the roof. The passenger side window lit up as one of the occupants hit a halogen searchlight. The harsh beam swept through the front of the building.

Kane pressed himself back into the shelter of the fire stair doorway. He was standing in a growing pool of blood and a dead body lay at his feet. It wasn't optimal. The searchlight played across the lobby. The beam struck the water in the fountain and seemed to intensify as the liquid reflected the illumination. As the light played past him, he listened for the sound of thundering feet in the stairwell at his back.

"Reaper? You copy?" Hennessey came over the radio.

"About time," Kane crypt-whispered.

Following the trajectory of the searchlight he crossed the lobby in a low shuffle and took a knee at the information counter. Cops to his left, stairwell to his right. The palms of his hands were slick with sweat.

"You got trouble," Hennessey said.

Kane almost choked. "You fucking think?"

"The cop in front of you is MOIS. Which means the guys in civilian clothes are maybe Department Fifteen."

Kane cursed, but didn't bother replying. Department 15 was somewhat analogous to the CIA's Special Activities Division, the branch filled with paramilitary operators. The Iranian unit were ruthless assassins and enforcers.

"But I got another MOIS uniformed patrol coming your way. They're being followed by a five-ton military truck. I'll show you my skinny white ass if there isn't an eight to twelve Revolutionary Guard death squad in the truck."

"I've got four to six in the building above me," Kane reported.

Outside, the driver of the patrol car got out. He wore an olive drab flak vest and held an H&K submachine gun on a 3-point tactical harness. The Iranian walked toward the front of the building.

"Shit!" Hennessey said.

"That doesn't sound good."

"I don't think it's part of the original response, but you've got Guidance Patrol headed your way too."

"Who the fuck is that?"

"Strictly second tier, basically religious police who make sure boys and girls don't dance. Think of them like the parents from Footloose, but with machine guns and APCs."

Kane paused. Men shouted from inside the stairwell. Out front the uniformed Iranian tried the door. He closed his eyes and sighed.

"APCs?" he repeated. "As in Armored Personnel Carrier?"

"Yes. An M one thirteen so old as dirt, but it's motoring toward you just fine. They've got a Soviet-era fifty cal mounted." The CIA agent paused. "I'm sorry, Reaper."

"We'll talk about it when I get out of here," Kane replied.

He turned off the radio, lifted his pistol and turned toward the stairwell door. Squatting down he put his back to the wall and took the grip up in both hands. The door opened inwards. An Iranian came through the door, submachine gun in his shoulder, muzzle up and tracking.

Kane held his fire as the man advanced in the room. A heartbeat later a second gunmen came through the door, tracking at a different angle, one that put him on a collision course with Kane's position. The PC-9 discharged twice, and the gunman's head jerked as a blood star spray painted the drywall. The man fell and the first gunman spun in surprise.

Kane shot him in the face.

The big Marine twisted around the edge of the doorway as the second gunman fell. The pistol was ready but there wasn't a third shooter in the stack. Kane twisted back, shoving the PC-9 away and yanking one of the dead gunmen's AKS-74Us up. He pivoted, still in a tight crouch as blood spilled out around his feet on the linoleum.

The police officer was trying to shout into his radio and bring his over H&K submachine gun up at the same time. Kane triggered a long, ragged burst of 5.45mm Soviet rounds. The hardball ammunition poured out on full rock-and-roll, green tracers knifing through the dim lobby. The bullets struck the one-inch thick glazed windows and chewed into them.

Boxing glove shaped holes punched through, leaving spider web tracks streaking out from the impact sites. Seven or eight of the rounds struck the policeman, hammering into his ballistic vest without stopping. The man shuddered under the impact like a toddler shaking a bowl of Jell-O and then pitched over backward.

The man's partner ducked behind the police car and began rapid firing his PC-9 pistol. Down the street the promised 5-ton truck rumbled into view. Like the punch line to a very bad joke, the M113 came in from the other direction only a moment later.

The policeman began shouting at the two vehicles and the machine gunner position in the turret on top of the armored personnel carrier swiveled his weapons toward the front of the building. Kane felt his eyes bulge in horror.

"Jesus Christ!" he snarled.

He shoved the door to the stairwell back open as the .50 cal cut loose. The cacophony of gunfire roared into the lobby of the building as the anti-materiel rounds bludgeoned through the front windows and slammed into walls, removing boulder-sized chunks on impact. The information desk came apart in splinters and sawdust. The fountain burst apart, and water jetted straight up from shattered marble fangs.

Out on the street the death squad began bailing out the back of the 5-ton truck, each of the eight men armed with an AKS-74U. The door to the stairwell swung closed and Kane charged up the steps.

Two men in olive drab uniforms and tan berets burst out of the second-floor entrance and onto the fire escape. They'd been focused on speed instead of possible contact and Kane took them down on the move. Hurtling past their bodies he went into a crouch and slid through the door from which they'd just emerged.

He saw the window at the end of the hall. Running on the fly he improvised. Sprinting, he contacted Hennessy.

"New plan," he shouted. "I'm coming out the back, second rendezvous point."

"In route," she answered.

"Expect hot," he warned, breathing hard.

"Yeah," she said, "I got that."

He lifted the gun and fired twice, blowing the glass out. Reaching the window, he began knocking icicles of glass clear to let him exit. Behind him the door to the stairs burst open and he spun. A gunman emerged, cut down AKS in his hands. The man cleared to the left and as he turned, Kane shot him twice in the chest.

The rounds staggered the man but the sound of impact on flesh was muffled and Kane figured he was wearing a vest. As the man fought to straighten up, he aimed carefully and shot him once in the face. The man went over and fell in front of the door.

Turning quickly, Kane threw a leg over the

windowsill, ignoring the crumbling shards of glass, and went through. He was two stories up and dropping to pavement. He was optimistic about his landing but went with the momentum the way he'd been taught in Airborne school.

His feet slammed the ground and he folded, rolling down along the length of his legs, somersaulting over a shoulder and coming up to one knee. Pain exploded in his ankle and he snarled at the sharp agony. Even as he fought to stand, he swept the pistol back up toward the window to cover himself.

He was in a wide, uncluttered alley running between the bank building and another high-rise. At the end of the alley a green and white police vehicle shot past, lights spinning, and siren wailing.

"I'm on the ground," he growled into the mic.

"Shut your whining," Hennessy snapped. "I'm about to take the corner."

True to her word, half a second later he heard the brakes on their car lock up and she skidded around the corner into the alley, tires screaming for mercy. Gunmen appeared in the window he'd just jumped through and he snap fired four or five rounds as Hennessy raced toward him.

He missed but the fire drove them back for a moment and the CIA officer skidded to a halt. Her arm shot out the open driver side window and she lobbed a smoke grenade toward him. He ran under its arc and heard it smack off the pavement behind him and begin hissing as it started spewing white-gray smoke.

He reached the car and she threw a second one.

The engine sang, the revs threatening to tear the hood off. Kane pulled the door shut behind him and was smashed back into the seat by the acceleration.

They cleared the smoke, slewing left into a tunnel between two blocks. The buildings whooshed by like brush strokes.

Kane punched the dash. Hard. The plastic split and his knuckle pushed out a ladybug of blood which he sucked away before speaking. "We were sold."

"Ya think?" Hennessey's sarcasm carved the air. She slung the car right. They crested the sidewalk, cutting a corner and then were out into wide open freeway. There were cars doing their thing in every direction. In twenty seconds, they were anonymous.

Kane felt like belting the dash again, but just sucked on the blood.

"Kohl. Only he knew what we were doing and where we were going."

"Great minds." Hennessy nodded.

"Find out where he lives. We're calling."

CHAPTER 12

Kohl's house was a minor estate. The bureaucrat's residence was in keeping with his cover as a successful international businessman.

Kane slid open the door and stepped inside. The house had the preternaturally quiet feeling of a museum or mausoleum. Everything was arranged for life to flow through this space; it was filled with potential energy, but no one was home. He closed the door after him.

This wasn't a fishing expedition, but he didn't know what he'd find, but it was far too convenient that the attack had come as it did. If Kohl wasn't compromised, then something didn't add up. Something was up. Checking Kohl's house was sound. No trust without verification. And Kohl stank.

He was inside the master bedroom. He stood still for a moment, getting a feel for the place. It wouldn't be out of the question for Kohl to have a CCTV surveillance inside his residence. Maybe hooked to his laptop, maybe his phone. Probably both.

For this reason, he'd worn the balaclava and bulky jacket. But even if he wasn't IDed, tripping video or some other silent alarm would greatly reduce his time on site. He needed to be focused, methodical.

"I'm in," he said. "Is our boy still tight in his office?"

"Target is at the restaurant we ate at with him, again."

Kane began moving around the room, checking in closets, under the bed, in desk drawers, behind paintings. He opened one door and found a spacious master bath. He tried the other and it opened onto the second-floor hallway.

"Who's at the meeting?"

"Facial recognition puts it as a minor functionary in the Ministry of Finance. I doubt it has anything to do with our op."

"Let me know if he suddenly acts like he's late for a very important date."

"Not my first rodeo."

"You do like your little jokes though." Kane chuckled.

He stepped into the hallway. Kohl had stamped his personality on the place in a way Kane found

mildly interesting. He'd taken the desert archi-
tecture of Middle Eastern influence and sifted it
through an American Southwest motif. The place
was terracotta tile and adobe-esque walls. Dark
wood, cut glass, and black metal furniture and
amenities. The rugs remained Persian, but the
color schemes were chosen for their similarity to
Navajo inspired palettes.

"That's true," Hennessy agreed. "Fat and Ugly
showing up pissed would be a pretty funny way of
saying *surprise.*"

"I know an entire SEAL Team who would find
you hilarious," he said.

"Is that some kind of cheerleader meets the foot-
ball team joke?"

"No, I mean they'd find you hilarious."

He descended a short, L-shaped staircase to
the first floor. He was operating on intuition. If
he hadn't found what he was looking for in the
upstairs master bedroom, he thought the next high
percentage location would be to see if Kohl had a
dedicated home office.

He trailed through a living room, still searching
for cameras. He didn't spot anything and walked
through an immaculate kitchen toward the front of
the house. There was a door at the opposite end of
the hallway set in the wall at the back of the living
area.

He tried the knob, found it locked.

"Curiouser and curiouser," he muttered.

"Got something?"

"We'll see."

He produced the lockpick gun. Pushing the tongs into the keyhole he flexed the lever and felt the mechanism click into place. He turned the gun and the lock slid back. He removed the device and pulled open the door.

Inside he found a room decorated more closely to Upper West Side Single Male than Persian or Navajo. The decor was incongruous. The home office screamed psychological "sanctuary" to Kane.

Kohl feels at home here, he thought. *He feels safe.*

If the counterintelligence chief was stupid enough, or more likely, *arrogant* enough to have anything incriminating, then Kane felt it would be here.

"Uh-oh." Hennessy said.

"Uh-oh what?"

"Our boy just picked up his phone scowled like he'd wet his pants, then called for the check."

"I think I just found his Bat Cave," Kane explained.

"Then do your duty and then boogie, 'cause it looks like Papa Bear is coming back to find out who's been eating his porridge."

"You just call me Goldilocks?"

"If the shoe fits…"

Kane entered the room. He was already burned, subtly was no longer an important concern. He needed to find whatever he was going to find and do it fast. Crossing to the desk he began rifling through drawers. He found papers, but a quick scan revealed them as personal documents. They might have held significance in a more general investigation but for a smash-and-grab info steal they weren't going to help Kane.

He pulled drawers out, checking their bottoms. He got down on his knees and looked beneath the desk. Not finding anything he moved to the book-cases.

"He's in his car and headed through traffic," Hennessy told him. "I'm hanging back but keeping him in sight."

Reaching up, Kane swept his arm and dumped a row of hardcovers to the floor.

"Don't lose him," he said. "I need to know when he's rolling up to the front."

"Even if we do, the GoPro we set up across the street will warn us when he pulls in. If he spots me tailing him then we're done for."

"You know what else could break our cover? If he breaks in here while I'm still looking, and I have to beat his ass like a redheaded stepchild."

"Why would the stepchild in this hypothetical situation have to be a redhead?"

"You're the brains in this outfit, supposedly. You

figure it out."

"My in-depth knowledge of the human psyche, and long experience as a ginger, leads me to believe you must want to commit some sort of aggressive action on my ass."

"Bingo," Kane muttered. His voice was deeply satisfied.

"I don't think you should be thinking about my undeniably shapely ass at the moment."

"Safe," Kane grunted.

"Safe? No, it's not really safe for you to be distracted right now."

"No. Jesus. I found a fucking *safe.*"

There was a pause. Then, "Ah, see, that makes more sense."

Kane dumped his backpack on his shoulder. He unzipped the top and quickly sorted through the hard plastic carry boxes in the black bag kit. Finding a medium sized case of the correct heft, he pulled out the electronic safe cracking device they'd taken from the safe house.

"What's the model?" Hennessy asked.

"S series, just like you suspected," he said. "You'd have thought he wouldn't have used commercial model."

"What's he going to do?" Hennessy asked. "Request an agency model? That wouldn't have raised a bunch of red flags? You're supposed to keep sensitive documents in the safe at the goddamn agency, not in your house."

"Good point," Kane grunted. "How's he look-ing?"

He opened the case and removed a thin black device shaped roughly like a windshield ice scraper a little larger than a Kindle. Hennessey had described it as the agency's version of the commercially available Little Black Box locksmith electronic safe cracking tool.

"Sonofabitch is making every red light," she re-plied. "But he's still ten minutes out."

"Good."

Kane produced a Spyderco Tenacious folding knife and used the thumb post to open the blade one handed. Using the tip, he prized off the face-plate around the electronic number pad, revealing a nest of red wires. Humming softly to himself, he pulled the four-wire system from its housing and slotted it into the modified Little Black Box. Once connected, he powered the device on.

The indicator light turned red, signaling the systems were communicating and Kane punched in the 5-digit access code to begin the system override. There was a pause, then the red light on the Little Black Box clicked off and the green bulb positioned next to it clicked on.

Grabbing the handle, he flicked it down and the safe door opened.

"I'm in," he said.

"Good," Hennessey immediately answered. "Because according to our Go Pro someone just pulled into Kohl's drive."

Kane straightened. "What? I thought you said I had ten minutes?"

"I said *Kohl* had ten minutes more to reach his house. This is another player."

Kane bent and began rifling through the safe. "Tell me when he makes it through the front door."

"Well, shit, isn't that interesting?"

"What? And I really shouldn't have to be asking 'what' in these kinds of situations. You should just be giving me the fucking information I need."

"Unbunch your panties, Reaper. It's the guy we saw in the hallway at Kathy Dansk's."

Kane whistled. "Oh, someone has some 'splaining to do."

"What's with the crappy Hispanic accent?"

"I'm doing Ricky Ricardo—you know what? Never mind."

He picked up the backpack and shoveled the safecracker into it. Keeping the bag open he began throwing everything he could find in the safe into the bag. He left several stacks of money in US dollars, Iranian rials, Euros, a 9mm SIG Sauer and four or five passports.

What he did shovel in was several manila envelopes and several folders filled with paperwork along with an iPhone. The communications device potentially held the promise of a treasure trove of data assuming they could crack it. From everything he'd seen so far, Hennessy was playing with some pretty cool toys.

"Asshat just breached the door."

Kane didn't bother answering. He heard the front door swing open and immediately sprang into action. Zipping the bag shut he threw it over one shoulder and produced the PC-9. He didn't know who the man outside the room was.

After sifting through all the evidence they'd just seized they could find Kohl was on the complete up-and-up and the alarm response by some kind of sanctioned diplomatic security attached. Then again, he could have just collected the goods to bring a traitor down and the fucker in the house with him end up being a paid assassin.

"Great job I've got here," he muttered to himself. "Kill him, don't kill him. Decide right now..."

He moved to the door and stood against the wall opposite the way the door would swing closed. He was anticipating a standard room clearing behavior on the part of whoever was outside. If he holstered his pistol that'd leave him both hands free to grapple and disarm, exactly what he wanted against a friendly operative. If he had his pistol holstered and things went poorly and the person outside was a bad guy, then he was dead.

Grimacing, he deliberately stuck his weapon

into his holster. He exhaled through his nose, forcing his body to relax into a supple, fluid state. Outside, the sound of footsteps stopped in front of the door. Kane studied the door.

The knob began gently rotating. Kane watched it turn until the latch clicked back out of the jamb. There was a pause. The body beyond the door shifted. Kane inhaled. He squeezed his hands into fists.

The door snapped open in a sudden motion. Two large hands encased in black leather gloves held a SIG Sauer in a double-fisted grip. The barrel was trained left as the person came through the door in a fast shuffle. Having cleared that vector, the weapon snapped around.

But Kane was right there, anticipating the other's movements like a dance partner. He grasped the weapon, left hand over the barrel, right hand tight against the hammer and slide catch. He twisted hard and the figure cried, the voice rough, male. Kane had the pistol.

The heel of a boot slammed against the former Marine's knee. Kane barked a curse as the leg folded. He didn't release his hold but twisted hard at the hips. There was a wet, organic *crack* and the man's trigger finger broke. The gun went off. Kane suddenly had it, all resistance gone, and he stumbled backward.

He caught his balance and made to rise and

turn the weapon when the masked figure shuffled forward and caught him in the chest just below his throat with an old school martial arts side kick that sent him flying backwards. His ass struck the desk and he came up short.

The man was on him, inside his guard. He ate an uppercut that knocked his head back. He tasted blood. A hooking body shot caught his liver and the SIG Sauer clattered to the floor. The man went for the gun and Kane used his heel to knock it under the desk. He brought an overhead elbow down in a twelve-to-six o'clock strike.

The blow smashed into the man and he staggered. Kane struck again. He saw the man's arm come back and knew he was trying for a groin strike. He shifted, catching the blow on his thigh. The man jumped backwards, and he produced a knife from behind his back.

It was a fighting dagger, slim, double edged with full tang and a blood groove. It wasn't a workman's blade. This was made for killing. When a potential enemy operative committed B&E against the Head of Station for Counterintelligence, then disarmed the security response using physical violence, it wasn't beyond the realm of reason that a good guy would think it was a life-or-death situation and respond with potentially lethal force.

If Kane drew his weapon, he could hold the man off. But to warn him back he'd have to talk. That could lead to identification. Identification led to a whole host of problems. Kane made his decision.

He pushed his legs into the ground violently and surged backwards over the desk. Rolling across the top he came down on the other side and snatched up the office chair. The man was lunging after him, arm coming across the distance with the knife stabbing forward.

The tip of the blade caught Kane along the back of one forearm as he lifted the chair. There was a flash of white-hot pain then the feeling of warm blood soaking his sleeve. Grunting with anger he heaved the chair full into the man's head.

The man stumbled back, and Kane vaulted the desk and leapt past him toward the door. Reaching the opening he took a look behind him and saw the man digging for his pistol from under the desk. Kane broke for the front door.

Racing down the short hallway he threw open the front door and sprinted outside. Rounding the corner of the residence he found the paved, semi-circular driveway. An adobe wall ringed the property and a wrought iron automatic gate on rollers permitted egress. The gate was open, and a blue BMW was parked in front of the house, the driver door hanging open. The assailant's vehicle.

He ran past it, heading full out toward the open gate. A fist-sized chunk of masonry erupted from the property wall in front of him. Almost simultaneously he heard the pneumatic cough of the silenced pistol. Without thinking he threw himself into a forward roll, somersaulting over one shoulder and throwing himself through the gate to place the wall between him and the man.

The weapon coughed three more times, all misses.

"Exfil is pretty fucking exciting at the moment," he transmitted.

"What do you need?" Hennessey responded at once, all trace of her usual hard ass bullshit gone.

"Just keep me updated on police response."

He turned the corner and saw his vehicle parked where he'd left it. He scanned the street. It was mid-afternoon, heading into the hottest part of the day and no one was on the street in the residential neighborhood. That didn't mean people couldn't be looking out their windows, but it encouraged him to keep moving at a jog.

Reaching his ride, he looked back. The man wasn't following him. Kane wasn't naive enough to think he'd made it. Pulling his keys free he thumbed the fob to unlock the car before getting in. He shoved his finger in the digital engine ignition and the car came to life. Ripping off the balaclava he looked in the rearview mirror.

Right on cue the blue BMW shot around the corner running like a stampede through a brushfire. Snapping off the parking brake Kane jammed the car into first gear and shot the gap around the front of the vehicle parked in front of him. He let the rpms scream up into the red, past four thousand, past five thousand, then speed-shifted through 2nd and straight into 3rd.

Engine still screaming he took the first corner that offered itself and snapped the front of the car to the right. He applied the emergency brake and slung his rear end around in a power slide that left half-moon crescents of rubber on the street.

Slicked, his eyes found the rearview mirror and he saw the BMW was right behind him. He cut the wheel to the left, refusing to engage the break before executing the maneuver. A car appeared in front of him and he swerved clear before the bumpers struck into each other. As he shot past, he caught an impression of an angry man screaming something.

Yeah, I don't blame you, buddy, he thought.

In the next moment a cacophony of car horns filled Kane's ears as his pursuer cut in front of the civilian driver who had to be convinced that the city had suddenly become insane. Kane gave it even odds that the man would call the police. The more they kept up the aggressive game of cat-and-mouse the more likely local law enforcement was to be drawn in.

He downed shifted as he approached a major avenue. Traffic was heavier here. It'd be easier to lose the tail, but it also greatly upped the chances of a bystander calling the authorities. Not bothering with his blinker, he turned into traffic and cut across two lanes. A discordant symphony of horns trailed behind him.

"Situation update?" Hennessy cut in.

"Making friends," Kane replied.

His eyes cut up to the rearview mirror again. The BMW was right behind him. Even as he watched, the low-slung vehicle shot around a white sedan, passing on the left, and surged toward him.

"Oh, fuck *you*," Kane muttered.

"What?" Hennessy asked.

"Tell me Kohl is nowhere near this," he snapped. He pushed the car up past 80mph.

"Yeah," Hennessy replied, "about that…"

"What?"

"He shot past the turn off to his house and is driving like mad for what I can only assume is the on-ramp to the freeway."

"The bastard tailing me is sending him instructions," Kane said.

"What's your plan?"

"I'll get back to you."

Up ahead he saw a break in the traffic. Across the median, traffic, while light, still raced past at freeway speed. If he mistimed this, he could flip his rig. In doing so he could take out innocent bystanders.

"I prefer my operations a little clearer cut," he snarled.

Adrenaline flooded through him, sending his heart skipping hard against the post of his sternum. Time slowed as he went into action. Left hand gripping the steering wheel at the eleven o'clock position, his right floated down and snatched up the emergency brake.

Even as his rear tires locked up in a screeching wail, he cranked the wheel hard counterclockwise. The rear end spun around, inertia almost lifting the chassis off the ground. His foot hit the clutch to avoid stalling the engine out and his car navigated a succinct 180-degree turn, smoke from the melting rubber of his tires filling the air like a dumpster fire. Inertia threw him backward into the seat, his lap and chest belts digging into him like vices. He gasped for breath as he fought the feelings of vertigo.

The car jolted hard, whipping his head around, as it drifted sideways and hopped the cement divider between directions of travel on the freeway. The vehicle came down hard and, foot still buried to the floor on the clutch, Kane shifted down into 2nd and hit the changing rpms in a ragged shift that made him think the transmission was going to drop straight out of the engine.

His foot came up as his other pushed the accelerator and his tires spun. The car lurched forward, and he slammed it into 3rd, tachometer still buried in the red. He shot ahead, going zero to forty in a handful of seconds.

Car horns blared as other drivers, heading directly toward him swerved out of the way.

He slalomed across the road and swerved into the breakdown lane. Once there he punched it and shifted through fourth to fifth gear. Cars zoomed past him in the other direction, moving so fast they were blurs of color. Up ahead he saw an off ramp. He checked behind him.

The tail was gone.

If he could avoid any police or killing someone in a head-on collision, he'd made it. Maybe.

"I'm clear," he barked.

"I'm going to your twenty," Hennessy assured him. "But you've got to ditch that vehicle. The police scanner is blowing up."

Kane hit the off-ramp doing better than sixty miles per hour and hugging the inside. A semi-truck came floating around the curve and he inched over until the retaining wall ripped the passenger side mirror from his door. Sparks flew in rooster tails as he scraped the paint from the vehicle. Two inches from his shoulder eight thousand pounds of truck and loaded trailer cruised past him.

Half an inch either way and he was jelly he knew. He felt like he was having a heart attack.

"I'd rather be shot!" he gasped.

He cleared the trailer and came up on the overpass. Cutting across three lanes he jumped the divider and got in the correct lane. He didn't even notice the cacophony of angry horns now. Looking around he quickly rattled off his address to Hennessy.

"Ditch the rig and get inside," she told him.

"Good copy that," he almost laughed. He hadn't experienced that much adrenaline since the first time he'd parachuted.

CHAPTER 13

The documents from Kohl's safe were mundane and uninteresting for the most part. Nothing that would incriminate Kohl like a searchlight in the darkness freezing him escaping against the prison wall. But there were deeds to a house, a hundred miles west of Zehedan in the desert that had sent needles bending on the screens of Hennessy's research elves.

"It's not on any of his registered property lists with the agency," Hennessy had said, plopping the file down on the table in front of Kane in the hotel room.

Kane leafed through. "Keeping things secret from the secret keepers paints an even more suspicious profile. The more I find out about Kohl, the more I don't like him. I take it he's gone to ground?"

"He hasn't been seen since we lit out of his residence."

"So, a secret house, out in the desert seems like it might be a reasonable place to start looking for him?"

"Yes."

Kane considered for a moment. "Or it might lead us to someone else…"

Hennessy nodded. "You thinking Clark? Midnight? Both?"

"I'm thinking all sorts of things." Kane got up. "I say we get going…"

Hennessey put a hand on his chest and pushed him back onto the bed and climbed on. "One battle at a time, soldier."

"Bingo," said Kane.

Satellite imagery gave Kane a couple more bingos on the way out of Zahedan. Hennessy showed him her phone screen as he drove.

In the dusty compound next to the house revealed in Kohl's safe, a white Mercedes with dirty windows.

"Clark's car?" Kane said, flicking through the intel in his mind. "The last car he was registered as driving?"

"Yup."

"Any sign of Kohl?"

"Not as yet but this other vehicle is potentially

even more interesting. To you at least."

Hennessey cycled through six images of a black Toyota sedan pulling into the compound in a cloud of dust. A door opening, a figure getting out, running into the house, face obscured. A figure, in black, like the car, and female.

"Midnight?"

Hennessy shrugged. "The elves didn't get enough of her to run facial recognition, but, it's a possible for sure."

"How long ago is that image?"

Hennessey checked the metadata on the capture. "Twelve hours, give or take."

Kane felt his foot pressing just a little harder on the accelerator.

The wadi where the house was situated was a dry riverbed cut into the edge of the plateau. The stream contained water only during the rainy season. They pulled the vehicle off the side of the road and killed the headlights. Hennessy, who'd taken over the driving so Kane could get his kit ready, shut off the engine and sat for a moment listening to the engine tick as it cooled down.

Through the windshield they had a good view of the backside of the plateau. The wadi climbed it like a scar. Above them the sky was clear and open, a quarter moon hanging in a myriad of stars. There was no cloud cover whatsoever. It was a horrible night for infiltration.

The lights in the compound at the top of the plateau blazed out into the desert.

"Well," Hennessey said, voice quietly sardonic, "they might see you coming from a mile away, but even if you aren't likely to get lost."

Kane smiled. He put a hand on her arm for a moment, something passing between them.

"We've talked about it," he said. "We have to go now. We wait for them to get one of my SEAL Teams into position, and Midnight, if she's there, could be gone, and with her, my route to the Black Swan. It's now or scrap everything."

"Some things aren't worth your life," she said, eyes dropping to the sand, like she meant it.

"You getting soft on me?"

"Your mom got soft on you," she snapped back.

Despite himself Kane couldn't resist the sudden surge of affection he felt for the foul-mouthed CIA officer. He slid his hand down to hers and lifted it to his mouth. He kissed her skin gently.

"It's simple," he said. "A little meet-n-greet, nothing more. I'm just going in the backdoor because Clark is jumpy and likely to run."

She turned to face him. "Midnight is going to be high strung and stressed as hell right now thinking Kohl is after her. That's the kind of situation where Russians kill everyone and then ask questions."

"So, I'll be better than them," Kane said.

Hennessey smiled. "No," she said. "*We'll* be better

than them."

"Let's do this," Kane suggested.

"Okay, Jarhead. Time to rock out with your cock out."

As Kane laughed, Hennessey popped the trunk and they got out of the vehicle. Kane was dressed for a night infiltration, but in civilian clothes in case they were stopped by law enforcement on their way to the site. Cruising southern Iran dressed like a ninja had never been an option worth considering.

When night fell the temperature dropped fast. Kane wore expensive, dust brown cross trainer hikers with trekker soles, tan Carhart pants; under a rugged button up flannel of brown and tan he wore a dark long sleeve shirt designed to cling to his frame. An OD green kufiyah was tied around his neck. He wore a tan baseball cap backward over his head and thin Isotoner gloves.

At the back of the vehicle he began putting on his kit. He shrugged into a London Bridge Trading plate carrier body armor and strapped it in. In the front pouch he secured three magazines for his primary weapon. Around the side were several utility pouches where he kept flash bangs, tourniquets, weapon retention devices for when he needed to climb, and drop pouch with a PRC 152 radio.

He strapped down his PC-9 to his leg and a 10mm suppressed H&K Mk23 in a shoulder rig. Hennessey stood silently, watching the road, as he fitted the four-tubed GPNVG-18 night vision goggles into place. After running a brief field diagnostic to make sure nothing had shifted during transport, he flipped them up and unlocked the case containing his primary weapon.

He lifted the MK18 CQBR with 10" barrel. Slapping in a magazine he snapped the dust cover closed over the receiver for travel and clicked over to 'Safe' before securing it to a three-point harness. Knife, multi-tool, the lockpick gun, and several zip-ties along with a field trauma kit rounded out his equipment. He'd debated bringing Round Defilade Optics in the form of a flexible fiber-optic camera and display but opted against the weight.

Midnight and Clark were home. He could feel it with the certitude of a long-practiced hunter. The spies had led him a merry chase, but it was time to close the race out. He shut the trunk.

"I'm good to go," he told Hennessey.

She nodded. "I'll get the drone up and be in overwatch."

They bumped fists. Kane used his thumb to shift the fire selector switch off 'safe'. He crossed the road and disappeared into the darkness.

CHAPTER 14

Jogging across the road he entered the wadi at the base of the plateau. Slowing as he picked his way across the broken terrain, he maintained a brisk pace, travelling by the moonlight. He went to step past a knot of brittle sticker bush and froze.

The cobra slithered out of the roots and lifted its head, the snake's hiss startling him with its volume. Kane jumped back in surprise and his heel caught a loose rock. He went down hard, the impact jarring up through his body hard enough to snap his teeth together. He had the Mk18 up before he landed.

The cobra slithered forward in a rush and he snap aimed, pulling the trigger on the carbine to fire from the hip. A three round burst ripped out of the M4-2000 suppressor and the head and hood of the cobra disappeared in a spray of black blood. The snake flopped to the ground like the mooring rope of a ship, heavy and loose.

"Jesus," Kane whispered.

"Reaper, are you in contact?" Hennessey came over his ear jack.

"Negative," Kane answered. "Fucking cobra..."

"I know you special operations guys are supposed to be snake-eaters, but now's not the time."

Kane snorted. "Reaper out."

He got to his feet. He shook his head, trying to clear his mind from the surrealistic shock of the sudden encounter. Reaching up, he snapped the night vision goggles into place and powered them up.

"Fucking cobra for Christ sake," he muttered.

He studied the top of the plateau for a moment taking in details. The location was typical of rural Middle Eastern compounds in that it contained a main residence of several stories, a handful of additional buildings and a courtyard surrounded by a ten-foot-high adobe-style wall. A single road wound up the opposite side of the wadi. Whoever commanded the top of the plateau would see someone coming for miles.

Kane moved with single minded determination. He had a schedule to keep and cobras notwithstanding, he was behind his timetable. Soon the wadi channeled him into a corridor of raw earth and exposed roots. As he began climbing, the obstructed depth perception of the NVGs became a hazard. After only a little while climbing, Kane was forced to disengage the night vision device or risk falling.

The way became steep enough that he was forced to secure his rifle and climb hand-over-hand. It was slow going and he was covered in sweat by the time he pulled himself over the lip of the wadi and onto the southern exposure of the plateau. He lifted the plastic hose for his CamelBak hydration pouch and sipped water. After a moment he keyed his comms.

"Reaper in position."

"Good copy," Hennessy replied. "I show no incoming traffic."

"Copy," Kane replied. "Reaper out."

It was time to go to work.

———————

The gully flowed into a culvert that ran beneath the wall to the compound. In the rainy season flash floods were common and could damage the foundations of buildings that had withstood exposure to desert heat for generations if not properly engineered against the sudden erosion.

Squatting down, Kane looked through the culvert. Remembering the cobra, he clicked his GNN-VGs into place and inspected the tunnel. Reaching up he hit the IR illuminator and turned his head slowly back and forth. He wasn't only concerned about snakes. Scorpions proliferated the area, including the deadly amber-colored Death Stalker. For that matter deadly creatures aside, the last thing he wanted was to belly crawl into a nest of camel spiders.

Each end was covered by a large mesh of steel wire. The stream bed was dry and large amounts of organic debris had gathered against Kane's end of the pipe where gravity had led water out of the compound during the rains. The mesh was covered with sticks, loose grass, and small branches.

Taking a pair of 8-inch mini bolt cutters from his LBX he began snipping the wire mesh loose where it joined with the aluminum alloy of the culvert pipe. He worked steadily, methodically.

"Do you have eyes on compound?"

"Affirmative," Hennessey answered. "No movement."

"Copy, Reaper out."

Finishing with the bolt cutters he bent the mesh back and peeled it down. Using the leg to which he'd attached his tactical pads, he placed a knee to hold the wire in place. Carefully he took the Mk18 up and leaned forward, pushing himself down onto his belly. Holding the weapon carefully, he began crawling forward.

The knee pads and boots protected him from the worst of it, but his elbows were raw and sore by the time he made it through the culvert. The entire crawl he kept picturing the cobra. Once something large with a lot of legs scuttled over his head and down his back, he managed to forget about the cobra.

Reaching the other side, he suppressed his natural urge to begin cutting his way out and scanned the courtyard. The space was hard packed dirt, baked flat as cement from the unrelenting desert sun. A car, a blue Audi four-door sedan sat parked across the way. The car sat between a two-story house and several modest outbuildings. Lights shone in the main house.

He studied the outbuildings as he used the wire cutters. They remained dark and silent. It was quiet enough that the sound of Iranian cicadas chirping outside the compound walls sounded loud. He snipped the last wire and pushed the barrier free.

He cleared out of the culvert in a smooth fast motion, freeing his weapon and bringing it up. He found the edge of the building, took a knee and cleared more vectors. Now, just beyond the Audi he saw the shadowed lee of a door. According to Hennessey's intelligence this was a side door leading into a kitchen area.

Carefully, he eased the rifle down and drew a pistol from the rig under his shoulder. Unlike the PC-9 on his thigh this one had a suppressor attached and was loaded with hollow point 9mm Parabellum ammunition. He keyed up his comms.

"Reaper going dark."

"Copy."

Snapping the NVDs into place he peered through the panoramic vision, seeing everything in the green tones of night vision tech. Weapon up, he started across the courtyard, passing the Audi and making a beeline for the door predetermined as his ingress point. Coming up to the door he took a knee and let his primary weapon rest.

He tried the handle. Door locked. Pulling a short, comma-shaped high carbon steel pry bar from his gear, and without preamble, inserted it into the door jamb and cracked it open, throwing it down even as the door swung open. He brought up his M4 and painted the interior with an IR spotlight on his Picatinny rail.

A short hallway was illuminated. Bare of everything except a coarse woven rug for scuffing the bottoms of feet, it ended in a short flight of steps and a closed interior door. Kane slipped inside, pulling the outer door closed behind him.

There were times when performing urban direct action that he lamented the switch from submachine gun to carbine as primary building assault tool. Rifle calibers were undeniably better for putting bad guys down, but the light, compact nature of the MP5s he'd initially trained on had their positive attributes as well, even though firing the smaller pistol cartridges.

He shuffled forward. Keeping his weapon

trained on the closed door before him, he tested the step with one foot. It was molded adobe, much like the exterior of the building. It took his weight without noise. He moved silently up, found the door unlocked, and entered a modern kitchen area.

The lights in the large room were off, but down a short hallway across a countertop from him, interior lights blazed. Sparing his optics, Kane reached up and snapped the sight upward. He scanned slowly, listening for sound. He heard nothing.

Creeping forward he skirted a restaurant-sized oven range, Maytag dishwasher and a generous wine rack. Devout followers of Islam did not seem to reside here.

He cleared the downstairs without finding anyone. Entry way, study, living area where a 72" television hung on a wall. He wove his way through furniture of all types and made toward the staircase to the second story. Still no noise.

He mounted the stairs, weapon ready. It occurred to him that either this was a trap, a false lead, or that the targets had relied upon not being discovered rather than traditional defenses. He supposed the relative remoteness of the compound could give the illusion of anonymity to those inclined to want to see it. Being on the run was an exhausting activity. He reached the top of the stairs.

The hallway before him stretched in either direction. To his left one wall was replaced by a railing, turning it into a balcony that overlooked the formal dining area. At the end of the corridor past several closed doors, one room showed a light under the door. Crouched, Kane moved toward it.

Approaching the door, he heard a sound for the first time since entering the house. He stopped, making sure he was hearing what he thought he was hearing. Cocking his head to one side he listened.

"Oh, Jesus Christ..." he muttered.

He opened the door and shuffled through, weapon up. His finger lay along the guard as he assessed the situation. On the bed two figures he recognized as Clark and Midnight. The Persian intelligence broker and gun for hire, straddled the CIA analyst like a Texas cheerleader on a mechanical bull. She looked good doing it.

"Seriously?" he asked. "Cliché much, Clark?"

"Cliché much?" Hennessy asked. "Oh! Damn! You mean..."

"Not now, Hades," Kane murmured.

On the bed Midnight threw herself off the befuddled Clark. Her movements were lithe and assured and Kane confronted the fact that getting the drop on a mercenary was always a dicey proposition. He snapped his muzzle toward her and barked out a warning.

"Stay down! Down!"

He cut loose with a 3-round burst that punched

into the mattress half a foot from Clark's head, the American froze, hands showing, erection wilting. Side stepping through the door to get a better angle, Kane swept his muzzle after Midnight.

"Show me your hands or I put your brains on the wall!"

There was a moment of stillness. Kane adjusted his aim. From this angle he could put a round through the edge of the mattress and directly into Midnight if he needed to. She had about half-a-second to surrender or that was what was going to happen.

After a moment, two female hands appeared.

"Merde," a husky contralto muttered in French. "Don't shoot," she added in English.

"Get up slow."

"I'm naked."

"Whose fault is that?" Kane snapped. "Now stand up."

Slowly she rose. Kane adjusted his opinion; she wasn't beautiful, she was stunning.

"At least let me give her a sheet!" Clark protested.

Kane nodded. "Do it. And put a pillow over your junk. That's nothing I want to see."

Kane waited as they complied, alert to subterfuge. There was none. He had them dead to rights and at a psychological disadvantage. Midnight watched him with cool, appraising eyes. It made him think she was trying to decide where best to put a knife, throat or groin? Clark made to start talking and Kane shook his head sharply.

"No, you listen now. I'm going to want some answers. I don't have to like the answers, but they better damn well be ones I believe. *Capeesh?*"

When they both nodded, he went on.

"Clark, there are more than a few people curious about where you've been. Think of me like animal rescue; I'm here to take you back to the pound." He jerked his chin toward Midnight. "And you, wow, what a very popular lady you are; just a real belle of the ball. So maybe we'll start with you."

"I want to defect," she said. "Clark was helping me."

"It's true," Clark echoed.

His voice was so sincere it cracked when he spoke, which most likely only meant that he believed what he was saying, not that what he was saying was actually true. Still, when the information matched up to his concerns about Kohl...

"So why didn't you?" he asked.

"In a word?" Clark said. "Kohl."

"The pig!" Midnight spat the word.

"Even though he's loaned you his house to keep you away from prying eyes? You're not ones for gratitude, are you?"

"He's burned us, or you wouldn't be here. There's only one reason you're here, because he wanted you," said Midnight.

Kane considered. She could be right. There was fuck all else in that safe of interest, other than the route to this house where Clark was staying. Had he and Hennessey been played?

"You getting this, Hades?"

"Fuck, yes. Slimy bastard. You thinking what I'm thinking?"

"That he wanted us all here at the same time? Take us out of the game in one play?" Kane spat into the mike.

Kane shook his head and felt like kicking his own ass.

"Ok," he said to Midnight and Clark. "We're on limited time."

Midnight's nudity was starting to become a distraction. Kane lowered his weapon, still ready to respond if needed. His finger lay along the trigger guard. He eyed them. Midnight was an accomplished liar, he could reasonably discard whatever she said, but he needed answers and he needed them quickly.

Clark was a different matter. Ostensibly he'd run agents and conducted security investigations but mainly he'd held his position due to technical expertise. He'd understood the science coming out of the Data Institute and doing so gave him introspection on where security leaks might arise.

Kane watched Clark. "What about Kohl?" he asked.

Clark met his gaze with a level one of his own. "Kohl's been running Black Swan alongside the DEA. Only he's used the relationship to facilitate his own off the books activities."

"Like what?"

"Like heroin trafficking and arms dealing," Midnight cut in.

"You have proof?"

The mercenary nodded. "I worked with Black Swan extensively. As a result, I was privy to Kohl's dealings. Once I was aware of him it was easy to know where to look to find out what he was up to. Kohl is a greedy pig. Black Swan's people hated him. I, on the other hand, am a beautiful woman. They loved bragging about what they'd do to me."

No wonder Kohl wanted them all erased.

She smiled. It was dazzling. He could almost feel her charisma in a tangible way, like the heat and glare of an intense search light. He could well imagine savvy criminals, let alone unsophisticated thugs, falling for her act. It was tier 1.

He forced himself to look away. He met Clark's eyes again.

"This true? You have proof?"

Clark grinned like a kid. "She caught him on video, wore a body wire, took screen shots from Black Swan's phone. We have Kohl fucking dead to rights." His grin melted. "Except the part where we couldn't get out of the country or contact Langley.

We're cut off, isolated, without resources or help. Kohl's too well connected."

"Not from me he's not," Kane said. He worked his comm with Hennessy. "You pick up what they just said?"

"Affirmative."

"I want you to get in contact with Melissa Smith. Use Reaper designation. We have to try and circumvent any safeguards Kohl may have built into agency official communications. It also looks like this might have become an extraction operation."

"I think that's called mission creep," Hennessey said. "Tell me they know where the fuck Black Swan is."

Kane looked at Midnight. "Can you give me Black Swan?"

Click. Flash. Midnight flashed her megawatt smile. "I can give you him wrapped in a pretty pink bow."

"Good." Kane went to communicate with Hennessey when Midnight cut him off.

"As long as we can come to terms…" she added.

"Wait one," Kane signed into his comm, "Hades, can you authorize this? I can promise to get them out, but I'm not in a position to negotiate terms."

There was a brief moment of silence. Just as Kane was about to repeat the question a voice broke squelch on the other end.

"I think you'd better consider the matter very

much closed," Kohl said.

Ice water pumped through Kane's veins as he recognized the voice and implications of it speaking to him through Hennessy's comms. He swallowed, riding the sudden surge of rage-adrenaline. When he spoke, his voice was rough but calm.

"Why don't you come up here so we can discuss this face to face?"

"Oh, I'm on my way."

The line went dead. Cursing, Kane stripped the comm unit from himself and threw it on the ground. Both Midnight and Clark watched him in amazement and confusion. Kane dropped the muzzle of his carbine.

"Looks like your luck ran out," he said matter-of-factly. "Kohl just shut down my backup. That means he knows where you are. I would assume he's got some narco-mercs with him to tie up loose ends." He paused. "In case it's not clear it's you two who are the loose ends and by 'tie up' I mean kill and bury in the Persian desert."

"They found us through you," Midnight said. She seemed to accept the fact calmly.

"You brought them down on us!" Clark accused.

"Likely," Kane admitted. "Our comms must have been compromised, maybe from the beginning. I don't know. I didn't exactly roll into Iran on the trail of a global drug dealer and expect to find a spy looking to defect, a CIA analyst willing to betray his oaths to help her, and a scumbag deputy station chief." He shrugged. "It is a little out of the ordinary, you have to admit." Letting his weapon rest, he clapped his hands hard. "Chop-chop, people. Get some clothes on, arm yourself and let's try and escape before criminal gunmen show up and slaughter us all."

"You sonofabi—" Clark started.

"Clark," Midnight cut him off. "Get dressed. We don't have time. I've told you what Kohl is capable of."

Clark shut his mouth. Still holding a pillow over his crotch, he reached for his pants and awkwardly began stuffing his legs into them. Midnight dropped the pillows covering her body and unselfconsciously began dressing.

It was easy to be unselfconscious when your body looked like that, Kane allowed.

"Vehicles?"

Midnight was almost dressed. "We have a CJ7 Jeep in the garage. It won't corner as well as the BMW but if we run into rough road it'll be better. Besides," she added, "it'll be easier to return fire from it."

"Good. Let's get the keys and get out of here," Kane urged. "I saw the alarm system coming in. Failing grade on that obviously. But do you have camera arrays?"

"On the front door and drive," Clark answered,

shrugging on his shirt.

"What do I call you," Midnight asked.

"Kane," Kane replied. He had no reason to hide his name.

"Ok, Kane," she said. "I'm going to open that closet. Inside are our weapons. Are you good with me arming myself?"

Yeah, good question, he thought to himself. He only considered saying no for a moment, the situation was the situation.

"Have at it," he said out loud.

Midnight nodded and immediately reached in grabbed two US issue plate carrier body armor rigs, each with two magazine pouches attached. She threw one to Clark who began putting it on. She reached into the closet and pulled out two folding stock AKS-74s. She expertly checked the assault weapon and primed it for action.

"Show me the cameras," Kane said.

"Follow me," Midnight answered.

CHAPTER 15

In an alcove off the entryway to the main foyer of the three-story building. Four monitor screens were attached to the wall showing the view directly before the front door, the drive, and just outside the gate. The fourth showed the rear of the house. When he saw that view, Kane realized he'd missed a camera on his infiltration. If someone had been monitoring these screens full time he could have been discovered.

"That's not good," Clark said, voice soft.

Midnight cursed in what Kane thought was French. He felt like cursing himself. Armed men had taken up positions around the gate, the headlights of their vehicles showing through in brilliant glare on the night optic camera feed.

Kane pulled his Iridium model sat phone. It was encrypted and quite powerful. He thumbed it on, entered 00 then the country code and the number he was attempting to reach. The phone gave him a screech of garbled static. Seeing the battery was green he scowled and thumbed it off.

"Jamming us," he muttered. "Figures. But I had to check."

"What now?" Clark asked.

He sounded nervous. Kane didn't exactly blame him. He counted roughly twenty enemy gunners. He was feeling a bit tense himself.

"Maybe we can make a deal," the analyst suggested.

"If Kohl wanted to negotiate," Midnight said, "he would have done so immediately. Kane is correct, he needs us dead."

"So," Kane sighed, "any of you ever watch Butch Cassidy and the Sundance Kid?"

Midnight frowned. "That's a movie?"

Clark groaned. "Yeah, they get slaughtered at the end."

"I hold to the historical evidence that Butch survived and lived out the rest of his life in Washington State," Kane said.

"Sure," Clark agreed. "He played checkers with Bigfoot."

"Shouldn't we be moving?" Midnight asked.

Something flashed across the fourth screen. Kane pointed quickly, all focus and intensity now.

"There," he said. "That was what I was waiting for. I needed to know the rear security element's location. I didn't want us running to the garage and into an ambush."

"Where are we running now?" Clark demanded.

"Nowhere," Kane said. "They had us from the get go. We can't get our own vehicles out of the gate because theirs are in the way. We're going to have to whittle their numbers when they try and assault us, then commandeer one of their rides."

"Oh, man," Clark moaned. "We're going to fucking die…"

"Here they come," Midnight nodded.

Kane saw them. On the screen a three-man breach team crept toward the front door in a loose triangle formation, weapons up. Kane stepped back from the others and lifted his weapon. He jerked his head, indicating the stairs behind them.

"Fall back, find cover," he barked. "We're defending, we have the advantage even with their numbers."

As the other two scrambled to obey him he lowered his M4 and triggered a series of 3-round bursts through the door. Even with the suppressor the sound of the cycling weapon chattered in the narrow confines of the hallway. A deadly steel flock of Teflon coated 5.56mm rounds punched through the door and spilled out into the Iranian night.

Falling backward as he fired several more bursts, Kane glanced toward the security monitors. The lead gunman was down and not moving. The others scrambled for cover outside the line of fire coming through the door.

He looked to the front gate and cursed. A two-man team of gunmen jogged forward, one of them carrying a heavy PKM machine gun with attached bipod. The man holding the weapon flopped down on his belly and aimed down the barrel. Beside him the assistant gunner held loops of belt fed cartridges.

"Shit!"

Kane spun on his heel and sprinted back the way he came. After three steps he threw himself forward and slid to one side of the big staircase dominating the entry hall. Behind him the machine gun cut loose, and the gunner raked the house. WARSAW 7.62mm hardball rounds punched through adobe-style walls and hacked through the wood of the door.

Rounds shattered windows, tables, chairs, decorative vases, ripped pictures off walls and blew apart several clocks. Kane huddled under the hailstorm of fire, using the staircase for cover as best he could. He risked looking around and saw Midnight and Clark had made the second level. He recalled that the house was built like a fortress on the lower two levels, with only two windows facing out. On the third floor a balcony ringed the house on three sides.

Behind him he heard an explosion and then the

shouts of angry voices. The rear team had effected entry with a breaching device he realized. The two teams had to be coordinating their movement and fire because just then the machine gun tapered off.

Hearing boots on tile, Kane scrambled up the stairs. He saw Clark and Midnight crouched on the hallway. They didn't look happy and their fear made Kane suddenly miss his team deeply. Everything would have been better if they were with him.

"Take those positions!" he ordered in a low voice and jabbed his finger toward where he wanted them.

The stairway was open and allowed an unimpeded view of the entryway at the bottom of the steps from all upper levels. A low wall ringed space and Kane himself took up a position against it after placing the others. He pulled a fragmentation grenade from his web-gear and yanked the pin.

"Oh shit," Clark moaned.

"Got anymore?" Midnight asked in a whisper.

Letting his M4 dangle from the 3-point harness, Kane made a sharp chopping motion with his hand, demanding silence. He heard the rear entry team (he thought Axe would most likely find the term 'rear entry team' hilarious) moving forward. Below him the point man emerged into view. He was Iranian, dressed in civilian clothes with body armor worn over them. He carried an AKM outfitted with a 75-round drum magazine. A tidy black mustache that reminded Kane of Burt Reynolds and Snidely Whiplash's bastard child, rode his upper lip like a disco caterpillar.

Kane released the safety spoon on the grenade and began his countdown.

Considering the man, Kane wished he was holding his M4 so he could shoot the man in the face as punishment for the abomination. Instead he made a snapping motion with his arm and the grenade shot out. As it dropped it sailed at an angle so that when it landed, bouncing hard off the floor just behind the point man, it did so in the direction of the team behind him.

Even as the grenade dropped, the point man snapped the barrel of his weapon up to cover the staircase. Kane threw himself backwards as Midnight opened up with her AKS-74. The weapon fired 5.45x39mm ammunition instead of the more common 7.62mm used in most Kalashnikovs.

The lighter rounds still carried more than enough kick. As Kane ducked back Midnight unleashed with the AKS. Unsuppressed the assault carbine chattered loudly, the racket deafening inside the house. Shell casings poured out in streams of gleaming brass and bounced off the floor.

Kane swept up his M4 and leaned over the railing in time to see the point man hit the ground like a sack of loose meat. He flopped once and the grenade went off. Black smoke roiled out from behind the stair and obscured the entry way. Kane heard the front door come open as someone kicked it down.

He turned toward Midnight and Clark. "Let's go, move to the back of the house; we'll use the secondary staircase."

They moved quickly without argument or questioning how he knew the layout so well. The time for talk was long past. They hustled down the hallway leading to several bedrooms, if Kane's memory of the blueprints was correct. At the far end of the hall a second, smaller staircase led down to the kitchen area.

He took another grenade and tossed it down the stairwell just to keep the Iranians honest. Then he ran like hell.

———————

Clark was in the lead as they headed down the stairs. *He may not know his ass from a hole in the ground,* Kane thought, *but he's highly motivated to protect Midnight.* Maybe he'd get shot and save Kane the trouble of trying to figure out what to do with him.

In a sort of twisted karmic accident Clark took fire as he entered the kitchen. A Kalashnikov fired several times in rapid succession as an Iranian screamed something Kane didn't understand.

Clark staggered as his body armor took the rounds. Midnight jerked him clear then came around the corner at the bottom of the stairs with her weapon on full auto.

Still coming down the stairs, Kane shouldered his M4 and fired several rounds into the wall. Interior walls were not thick enough to stop bullets and his bullets would cut through the kitchen to add to Midnight's suppressive fire.

Reaching the bottom, he stepped over a panting Clark and followed Midnight into the room. Barrel smoking, the woman stood over a dead gunman. Her rounds had torn his jaw from his face and blown the back of his head out.

Nice, he thought. *If she can keep shooting like that, we might stand a chance.*

He turned back to Clark as Midnight covered them. Clark was alert, face twisted up in agony as he struggled to stand. There was no blood. He'd taken the rounds center mass where his ballistic plate stopped them, but he'd also taken them point blank and Kane could only imagine how much pain the man was in right now.

"Come on, Clark," Kane said, "we've got to move!"

To his credit Clark came when Kane pulled him. The analyst was game enough when the stakes were high. Midnight had her weapon trained on the opening leading to the hallway that ran toward the front of the house. Kane swept up his weapon and headed for the back door.

"Follow me," he barked.

He shuffle-stepped forward, reached the door and pulled it open. They halted for a moment as he took a quick peek around the corner. An Iranian with an AKM wearing a Liverpool FC Premiere League soccer shirt under a bulky OD green flak vest that looked left over from the Soviet invasion of Afghanistan.

He shouted in surprise when Kane's head snapped around the corner and brought his weapon to his shoulder. Kane dropped to one knee and leveraged the barrel of his M4 around the corner. The Iranian cut loose and 7.62mm rounds blasted into the sun-dried brick of the house. Shards of the adobe-like clay exploded in bursts of dust clouds and bullets hissed past above him.

Kane fired several bursts as suppressive fire then peeked around the corner to try and draw down. The soccer fan was racing toward the cover of the BMW. Kane snap fired, missed, adjusted, and managed to put a 3-round burst directly in the sprinting man's path. The rounds clawed into his legs and the man screamed as he fell.

Kane swept his muzzle up the length of the man's body and snapped his fire selector switch off burst. With cool precision he put two rounds into the man's head. Brains splattered the side of the BMW.

"Let's go," he told Clark and Midnight.

CHAPTER 16

They left the house and Kane jogged them towards the culvert. He was thinking fast on the fly now. If Hennessy hadn't been compromised, he would have returned to their rally point and she could have driven them clear. There was no point in returning now. Either Kohl was waiting, no doubt with a personal security detail, or he'd take the CIA officer and moved to a different location.

Retreat wasn't going to work in this shit show he'd found himself trapped in. But he could make use of surprise…

"Toward the back wall, go!" he ordered. "We're going out through a culvert."

Clark was moving better, his face still twisted with pain. Kane wouldn't have been shocked to learn several of the man's ribs were cracked or broken outright. Crawling was going to be agony.

Beats the alternative, he thought.

They reached the culvert. Kane spun and pulled security, back to the opening.

"Go," he said. "Before they send more men up the side of the house."

"You want us to crawl into that black hole?" Clark gasped around the pain. "Are you fucking nuts? There could be scorpions or cobras in there! This isn't Fort Benning man; it's fucking Iranian desert."

"Come on," Kane argued. "What are the chances of there being *two* cobras so close together? They're very territorial."

"Wait...*two* cobras? What the hell does that mean?" Clark sputtered.

"Go," Midnight urged him. "Go or get out of my way. Kane's right, we don't have much time."

Kane plucked a smoke grenade from his web gear as Clark begrudgingly entered the opening. He pulled the pin and tossed the spewing canister under arm so that it rolled across the hard-packed earth of the courtyard. In seconds dense grey smoke began filling the confined area.

Have a little fog of war, Kane thought, feeling satisfied. Then an image of Hennessey in Kohl's hands flashed through his mind like pictures on a TV screen and the feeling of satisfaction vanished.

When he turned, Clark was already in the culvert and Midnight's feet were just disappearing through the opening. Wasting no time, he knelt and followed them back out through the culvert.

What a difference 15 minutes makes, he thought.

———————

Emerging out the other end Kane found Clark and Midnight pulling security. He'd have preferred having Brick and Cara, but he'd take what he could get at the moment, and at least their heads were in the game.

"Change magazines," he whispered. "Give me as accurate an account of how many rounds you have left, your physical state, and any damage to your equipment."

This was his version of a standard infantry ACE report post-engagement. ACE stood for Ammo, Casualties, and Equipment. The status of those three things helped determine the next course of action.

Both Clark and Midnight had been outfitted with three 30 round magazines. Midnight had 59 rounds left, Clark 84.

"Physical?" Clark repeated, voice somewhat incredulous. "Physical, I feel like a mule just tap danced on my chest. It hurts when I breathe...or move."

"But he's not bleeding," Midnight interrupted. "And he's not spitting up blood." She felt under his vest ignoring his wince of protest. "And there's no abdominal swelling. Maybe a cracked rib or two, bruising to the sternum." To Kane's incredulity she took Clark's hands in both of hers and spoke softly to him in a voice somewhere between a mother's encouragement and a bedroom whisper. This only served to make what she said next sound more surreal. "I'm going to need you to Cowboy Up now, okay, Teddy Bear?"

Clark blushed, but to Kane's surprise he also saw the man draw himself up straighter, take control of his pain. *Jesus,* he thought, *she's got his number dialed in pretty well.* Which only proved he couldn't trust them.

"I'm good, Midnight," Clark assured her. He turned to Kane, a new man. "Let's do this."

Kane sighed. He missed Team Reaper. Badly.

"Stay low and follow me," he told them in a low voice. "We're going straight up the wall to the front drive. We'll hit them from behind and unass this AO in one of their vehicles. If we have an opportunity, we disable their vehicles. Everyone understand?"

They both nodded.

He turned to lead them out and froze. He cocked his head, ear to the sky.

"That can't be good, right?" Clark said.

Midnight cursed in French.

"Oh, fuck me," Kane muttered to himself.

Approaching rapidly on a direct course for the

compound was a helicopter. Reinforcements were arriving. *Changes nothing,* Kane realized. *Nothing to it but to do it.*

"Let's go," he said. "We try and flee on foot they'll just hunt us down all the easier."

They began moving out.

Racing the helicopter, they moved up the side of the compound. On the edge of the plateau they had to choose their steps carefully or risk falling. Each footfall caused minor avalanches of gravel. They heard men yelling inside the compound. Another team must have breached the house and were communicating what they'd found to those left outside. It was hard to tell how many men they were dealing with.

At the corner of the compound wall Kane halted and took a knee. Easing his head around the corner he surveyed the scene. Outside the gate were four vehicles, all running with their high beams on. There was a VW minivan on balding tires, two white Datsun pickup trucks, and a nicer Land Rover Kane immediately knew must belong to whoever was running this aspect of Kohl's operation.

Two gunmen in Soviet flak vests over civilian clothes stood security. They carried AKMs but their focus was on whatever was happen inside the compound. *Sorry Kohl,* Kane thought, *it's hard to find quality help that also murders on command when you try and freelance it. Asshole.* This take-down was looking very doable.

Midnight came up beside him. He pulled his head back and let her look. Crouching, she peeked around the corner. After a moment she leaned back.

"That Land Rover, right?" she asked. "Last in line, large enough to fit us all. Someone could return fire from the rear."

"Exactly."

This close to her he could smell her perfume. Unbidden the image of her bucking naked on top of Clark flashed through Kane's mind. Scowling, he pushed it away.

"Alright, here's how we do it," he said. "We hit them. I take those three out with my suppressed weapon. You two back me up in case something goes wrong. We all move forward. Clark and I cover the gate while Midnight secures the Land Rover. As soon as she's behind the wheel we get in, Clark into the back where you can return fire and me riding shotgun."

Clark, sour expression firmly in place, opened his mouth to begin expressing his displeasure at Kane riding next to Midnight. Knowing that was going to happen Kane reached out gave a short jab to his ribs through the body armor.

Complaint cut off by a gasp of pain at the impact,

Clark sagged. Kane caught him, free hand closing in a vice around the analyst's arm.

"No argument, motherfucker. I need her. I'll leave your ass behind if you don't do what I say when I say it." Kane leaned his face in close, every inch the schoolyard bully he needed to be to gain control of this situation. "Do we have an understanding?"

"Clark, *please,*" Midnight urged him. "We don't have time."

Clark jerked his arm free, refusing to look at Kane. He muttered something.

"What?" Kane demanded.

"Fine," he repeated. "I said fine."

"Good then let's go; we've got people to shoot in the face and I'm very excited to get started doing that."

"Lead the way," Midnight said.

Kane nodded curtly. The clock really was ticking, and its tick-tock was in the buzz of an approaching helicopter.

He started forward. His weapon came up and he snugged it into his shoulder and began searching for his target. He stepped smoothly, crouched, not crossing his feet over one another as he shuffle-stepped out from cover. For a moment there was an instant of apprehension as he realized his intended target had moved.

Then he found them. Harsh cough of his suppressed round. The bullet struck the oblivious man in the side of the head. A blood halo appeared briefly in the glare of the vehicle headlights then the man dropped.

Kane paused, shifted at the waist, found the second gunman. The man released a plume of smoke and flicked a cigarette away. Weapon cough. The man's head jerked like a speed bag and he fell.

The third man noticed motion out of the corner of his eye but wasn't yet alarmed. He turned to look behind him, questioning look on his face clear in the illumination of headlights. Kane shot him twice in the face and the back of his skull exploded outwards like shards of a broken dinner plate.

"Go! Go! Go!" Kane urged.

Midnight sprinted past him heading for the driver side of the Land Rover. Clark came up beside him and they swept their weapons toward the compound's front gate, covering against the possibility of men running back out.

"Come on!" Midnight called.

"Go," Kane ordered, "into the back and be ready to put down some cover fire, Go!"

Clark didn't argue for once and instead took off toward the vehicle. Kane followed him walking backwards, keyed up to fire. He knew he risked the chance of them driving off and leaving him, but it felt Midnight had grasped the truth that he was her last, best hope.

At least he thought so.

Above them a blue and white Bell 214 appeared. It was barely one hundred yards off the deck. A man in dark clothes held a SAW and leaned out of the open bay door, one booted foot on a skid. Clark made the Land Rover and flung open the back door, Kane half a dozen steps behind him.

An Iranian holding a pistol walked out of the gate, weapon in hand but not on guard. Kane shot him twice in the chest and once in the head when he was on the ground. The helicopter swung out around the area and started doubling back.

The jig was up, Kane knew. He raced for the Land Rover. As he ran, Midnight leaned across the front seat and threw open the passenger side door. Kane ducked into the vehicle at a run. The door wasn't even shut before Midnight, having the vehicle already in reverse, slammed her foot down on the gas and forced the Rover through a sloppy reverse spin.

The rig shuttered to a stop, front end pointing back down the road leading to the top of the plateau where the compound sat. Car vs helicopter wasn't Kane's idea of a great match up, but neither was escaping on foot.

"Clark, fire up their vehicles!" he shouted.

A moment later, the American intelligence analyst began cutting loose, firing directly out through the rear window of the Land Rover. 5.45mm rounds began chewing apart the sitting vehicles.

As Midnight floored it Kane leaned out of the passenger window and took aim at the helicopter. It was a civilian model and without armor upgrades, so it was conceivable that Kane could take it down even with just an assault rifle. Helicopters were powerful workhorses, but they also contained technical, finely-tuned balances of machinery that were armored in military models. Even a handgun round in one of those areas could play havoc with it.

Despite this, what Kane was really focused on was thwarting the SAW gunner. That threat could end their run in moments. Kane took aim, Midnight slewed around the corner throwing his shot wide. The helicopter swung out to flank them and put its nose down to make a run past them.

The door gunner opened up but Kane immediately saw that the man had no experience firing from a helicopter. Instead of firing behind the racing Land Rover and using the 'copter's speed to sweep the bullets into the target, he attempted to fire in front of the vehicle the way a stationary marksman would engaging a moving target. As a result, the bullets landed well behind them.

Kane knew exactly how to adjust between the two moving vehicles. Even so, the job was difficult and made more so by Midnight's driving. He triggered a 3-round burst which was promptly swal-

lowed by the desert night. Tried again and knew
he'd put it too far wide. Readjusting, he tried for
a third time. He saw sparks fly off the Bell 214's
nose and the helicopter suddenly swung wide. The
abruptness of the maneuver almost caused the door
gunner to lose his footing and his burst cut the air
well above the roof of the Land Rover.

"One of the cars is following us!" Clark shouted.

Kane, still hanging out the window, risked a
look behind them. A white Datsun pickup truck
was in pursuit. Three men stood in the bed of the
truck and laid their weapons across the cab roof.
Inside the vehicle a second man sat beside the driver and was aiming a pistol out the window.

"Shoot them!" Kane yelled.

Clark responded. The racket of his AKS going
off drowned out the helicopter for a moment. Bright
flashes of illumination spilled out of the windows
in cadence with his muzzle flash. Behind them the
truck swerved, and the other men returned fire.
Bullets cut the air around him.

Midnight was driving the Land Rover hell bent
for leather down the narrow dirt road cut into
the side of the plateau. The back end slipped and
slalomed as she took corners too fast, it was impossible for the shocks in the vehicle to compensate for
washboards and pot holes at these speeds. Several
times Kane was almost thrown clear of the window.

Finally, after the branches of a roadside tree slapped into him like leather whips, he relented and pushed himself down inside. The helicopter gunner had stopped firing when his rounds came closer to hitting the Datsun pickup than Kane and his crew. The Bell 214 shot past them about half a mile out and swung around.

"It's going to make a run straight at us!" Midnight shouted.

"Keep your eyes on the road," Kane shouted back.

Leaning out his window he drew a bead on the helicopter. If the pilot was going to keep it steady to help his gunner aim, then that meant it would be a steady target for Kane as well. It was a deadly game of nerves. Unlike the pilot though, Kane knew the fugitives in the Land Rover didn't have the choice to back down.

The car reverberated in a series of shudders as Midnight powered them through deep ruts cut into the road. Kane fired. The helicopter drifted off the center line on its approach, putting itself just to the right of the Land Rover and the gunner straight down the middle.

"Fuck! Fuck! Fuck!" Midnight screamed.

The gunner opened the SAW up.

Slugs ripped up the row and slammed into the grill of the Land Rover in a hail of lead. The slugs punched through the thin metal skin of the hood and ricocheted off the engine block. The windshield spider webbed then shattered in the middle as the line of 5.56mm rounds splintered the safety glass.

Kane felt the concussion of the burst as it passed between him and Midnight and ripped into Clark. Clark made an animal sound of agony as the bullets struck him in a succession of meaty *thwaks*. The man's scream strangled off and he went quiet.

The helicopter passed by them in a flash and Kane returned fire, forcing the gunner to readjust as the pilot swerved off again. In the brief reprieve Kane risked a look into the back. Clark lay motionless, sprawled against the back seat. His weapon had dropped into the back and blood leaked from him in rivers. He'd been struck in each leg, his gut, side and upper back. His clothes were shredded when the tumbling rounds created vulgar exit wounds.

"Is he dead?" Midnight asked, voice tight.

Air rushed in through the shattered window, desert hot and smelling of dust. Kane's body ran slick with sweat. Behind them the pickup tried to rush forward but Midnight put the Rover into a power slide that took them around a corner and cut them off from sight for a moment.

"He's still breathing," Kane said.

He turned to look out his open window, tracking the helicopter as it took a long loop. It seemed that this time it was going to come up their backside right over the heads of the Datsun pickup.

"I came up the backside," he said. "How far are we from the highway?"

"Two miles maybe," Midnight said. "Don't count on traffic chasing these guys off."

"I'm not," Kane grunted, "but I'm hoping for a smoother shooting platform."

"There's a bridge up ahead, over a relatively shallow dry riverbed," Midnight told him. "Maybe fifteen feet deep."

Kane twisted around and looked behind them. Clark was going to bleed out if he didn't get help soon.

"What's your point?" he asked.

"I think we'd stand a better chance by finding a defensive position."

She yanked the emergency brake and fishtailed around a sharp, right turn, took her hands off the wheel to let it correct itself, and then gunned the Rover forward.

"I understand why we had to flee the compound; they caught us by surprise and there were so many of them maneuvering we couldn't hope to keep track of them all."

Kane fired two 3-round bursts out through the back of the Land Rover. One of the headlights on the Datsun exploded and the driver stepped on the brake. Kalashnikov rounds burned around the car and the passenger side rearview mirror exploded like a bomb.

"Plus, you know, fucking helicopter!" With her accent the word came out *foo-keen*.

The Bell 214 roared over them but the gunner's burst raked the earth just behind them. Kane's mind went into overdrive, debating tactics. Midnight was correct that running from a helicopter hadn't been part of his original plan.

If they could get under the bridge for cover, they might be able to repulse the helicopter runs until low fuel or ammo drove them off. If that was going to work, however, that meant dealing with the gunmen behind them.

"Do it," he told Midnight. "Get our backs to a wall and heads under cover; this is a long shot but we're just too exposed right now. Soon or later that ass hat in the helicopter is going to get his range dialed in and then we're done for."

Midnight nodded, face grim, and stepped on the accelerator.

The truck behind them sped up and Kane pushed them back with controlled bursts through the blown out back window. His magazine ran dry and he changed it out just as the Bell swooped in from the side. Rounds hammered the Land Rover, punching like nails through the roof. One struck the ballistic plate in Kane's vest and he gasped in agony at the brutal impact. Rounds tore through the backseat, striking Clark's immobile body.

Midnight cried out and the vehicle swerved wildly. Kane looked and saw blood gushing from a wound in her leg where it was up against the driver side door. He leaned across and applied direct pressure, trying not to get in the way of her driving.

"There it is!"

At Midnight's shout Kane turned and looked. Through the spider webbed windshield, he saw the old Soviet era bridge. It was an ugly, sturdy monstrosity of concrete and asphalt.

Midnight slewed the car sideways and worked the brakes. They jerked to a stop in a cloud of dust and the vehicle rocked on its suspension. Kane and Midnight threw open their doors, a cry of anguish ripped from the woman as she put weight on her wounded leg.

"I'll get Clark," Kane shouted. "Go!"

She hesitated for a moment until she saw him open the rear door and yank the limp, unresponsive body of Clark out of the vehicle. She hobbled toward the cover of the bridge as Kane dragged Clark after her. Down the road the Datsun sped toward them and the helicopter swung back around for another gun run.

Midnight made the edge of the bridge and went to the side, slipping under it to take cover. The earth slanted downward at a steep angle to a dry riverbed but the slope was enough for them to find purchase and fire around the abutment.

Panting, body drenched with sweat, Kane dragged Clark toward safety. Rounds from the gunmen in the Datsun hammered the stalled Land Rover. Reaching the bridge Kane heaved, sending Clark's body sliding under the top decking of the roadway.

On the other side Midnight fired. Kane slid down on his belly and ducked under cover. As the helicopter swept past, he fired after it. The Datsun raced up the road toward them and a hurricane of bullets swept across the bridge.

As the helicopter swept back around, Kane took his last fragmentation grenade and tossed it underhand. The green, baseball-sized sphere arced out, bounced off the road and rolled under the Land Rover.

"Fire in the hole!" Kane shouted.

A moment later the grenade exploded under the Land Rover, splitting open the gas tank and creating a massive detonation that lifted the vehicle several feet into the air. Frame twisted and burning, the Land Rover came back down with a thump.

There was no way the Datsun was getting past that roadblock. The helicopter swept toward them. Kane twisted to put his sights on it in hopes of getting the door gunner. His finger froze on the trigger.

As he watched, Hennessy flew from the helicopter. He couldn't hear her screaming as she plunged down toward the bridge, but he saw the terror in her face as she fell. She struck the road between the bridge and the burning Land Rover with enough force to split her skin and sent her internal organs spilling out onto the ground. Her head bounced, and deformed; blood soaked her fiery red hair.

Kane heard an animal howling from somewhere but only when his voice cracked, did he realize he was the one making the sound. His breath was gone, and he couldn't seem to get it back. Hennessy wasn't just dead; she'd been smeared like fruit across a dirty road.

Circuit breakers existed to protect against current overloads in electrical devices. Under the right circumstances human beings have them also, in an emotional sense. Sometimes the weight of grief and rage grows too great for the system to handle and *snap* goes the breaker in their head.

Kane's breaker snapped over.

He climbed out from under the bridge and calmly started walking forward. He dropped his partially-spent magazine and slammed home another. He tapped the bolt release and felt the round seat in the chamber as he shouldered the weapon.

He wasn't consciously making any decision now. His body was acting of its own accord, operating on pure muscle memory. His mind felt like a passenger only tethered to his body. It was as if he were only a witness to the actions of his body. He didn't look at Hennessey's body as he swept past.

Coming around the burning vehicle he saw the Datsun parked in the middle of the road. He caught two of the gunmen as they leapt out of the back and began running forward. Shoot. Shift, pivot, squeeze. Shoot. The gunmen dropped to the ground, weapons bouncing on the hard-packed dirt of the road.

From over the back of the Datsun cab a Kalashnikov erupted into life, starfish pattern of muzzle flash illuminating the darkness beyond the burning car with a strobe light effect. He felt the concussive buffer of rounds burning past, heard the *hiss-spat* of the close calls.

He fell into a slow shuffle, keeping his weapon steady as he advanced. Kane aimed into the starring muzzle flash, caught a dark silhouette behind the weapon and put his rounds center mass. The gunman jerked sideways and flopped loosely against the man next to him.

Startled, the gunman pushed and the dead man dropped back. As the living fighter twisted back to fire, Kane shot him in the neck and face. On the road Kane skipped sideways, inserting the engine hood in a diagonal line between himself and the last shooter who was firing from behind the driver door.

The Iranian gunman fired, after a short burst his magazine went dry and he scrambled to switch it out. Kane was twenty-five yards from him by then. He stalked forward as the empty magazine fell to the man's feet.

The man looked up as his left hand slapped inside the pickup, looking for another magazine. Kane walked forward. The man's face shone with sweat and twisted in terror. He mumbled something to himself in Persian.

Finally, the gunman threw down his Kalashnikov and scratched for the pistol hanging under his chest. *Should have gone for that first*, Kane thought. *Now you die.* Kane's weapon spoke in an abrupt burp. The gunman's head collapsed inward and blood misted in a sudden violent spray that struck the windows and shards of windshield of the pickup.

In the silence that followed Kane heard the Datsun's engine running. Despite several bullet holes in the grill the motor sounded fine. Kane blinked, coming out of the fugue. He was a swimmer breaking the surface after diving deep. He heard Midnight shouting behind him and turned.

The mercenary had crawled out from under the bridge and was walking toward him. He looked at her, head still foggy as the adrenaline bled out from him. The burning Land Rover threw flames three stories high, but already the intensity following the explosion was dying down.

Midnight reached him, said something.

"What?" Kane asked.

"I said," she repeated, "why do you think the helicopter took off?"

Kane looked up. Some part of him had realized the Bell wasn't coming in for another run because he hadn't automatically turned to engage it. Consciously now he discovered the Bell had disappeared into the night and only the fading sound of its engine was left.

Kane shrugged. He was coming back into himself now.

"Kohl saw we were going to be too tough to kill. Or the door gunner brought a single two hundred round drum thinking that'd be enough. Either way," Kane said, "he's either going to go back and try and pin this on me or he's going to run for it."

"Can he pin it on you?" Midnight asked.

"Not a chance in hell my people will believe it," Kane said. "Not one single chance. He's going to have to run."

"What will you do?"

"Find him."

CHAPTER 17

Kane sat in the dim room waiting for the satellite connection to go through. Brick, fresh in from Mexico, sat next to him doing something on his iPhone. Kane saw Hennessy's body falling out of the helicopter and smashing like a pumpkin on the desert road. He blinked slowly, forcing the image from his mind. He let out a pent- up breath.

To distract himself he surveyed the room. Besides Brick there were other faces Kane knew well, men he'd worked with in the past. This operation had been so plagued, almost cursed, from the beginning and after the way Hennessy had gone out, he couldn't help but wonder which of the men now with him were also going to die.

Across from him sat Chief Hunt.

Borden Hunt, call sign Scimitar, was a *chew-it-up-and-spit-it-out-level* experienced Naval Special Warfare operator. He led SEALs into battle from the front, and his men respected him immensely, as did Kane. His average height and build belied his physical prowess. This was a man who could swim 5-miles of open ocean to cut a terrorist throat in the dead of the night.

Hunt had reported with two of his SEALs: Rucker, his corpsman, and Mike Oil, the team Designated Defensive Marksman. Rucker stood 6'1" and looked built to compete in Ironman races. Oil, whose call sign was Pop-Eye, was taller than Rucker by an inch or two and built like an ul-tra-marathon runner. Kane had worked with both men before and knew how good they were.

Sitting beside Pop-Eye, fingers working rapidly across the keyboard of his military laptop, was a member of the Worldwide Drug Initiative's "Bravo Team", Sam "Slick" Swift. Swift was the electronic counter-measure and cyber security wizard. Kane knew that General Thurston had felt it was essential to have him on this op, but it still made Kane nervous.

"Ten hut!"

Colonel Jameson Lord came into the room, his face freshly shaven, and his eyes like holes thumbed in the snow of his face. Lord was operations chief at Bagram, and he was here to brief Team Reaper.

"Seats please, Gentlemen."

His eyes flicked to Cara, who sat at the back of the room, back in uniform, arm in a sling, eyes still panda bruised, but straining at too many leashes to get back into this fight to keep her down long.

Kane had tried to talk her out of it, even just running shotgun for Reaper from cover, but she wasn't having any of it. "Team Reaper 'til I die," she'd told him.

"And *lady* gentleman," Lord acknowledged. "You've all been called in here because we have mission data for you. I assume you know why?"

"You've found them?" Kane was making fists below the table. It was the only question he'd been wanting answered in the last six days since getting back to Afghanistan with Midnight...and Hennessy's body bag.

"Yes. The Bell flew North West towards Turkey. We picked it up again on satellite nine hours later, heading west. They landed at Çukurova Regional Airport then transferred to a Gulfstream G550 that was waiting for them on the apron. That flew west again, landing at a private airstrip on the outskirts of Divjakë, Albania. From there, we're pretty sure—looking at listening station intel we have—they've gone out into the Adriatic, to *Kafka e Bardhë Ishull.* White Skull Island to you and me. Old fishing island. Sometimes used by Mafia from Sicily across the way, sometimes by Albanian gangsters as a smuggling stop off, and sometimes by RENEA on sanctioned operations. And we think this is one of those."

RENEA troops were elite Albanian police units operating with a great deal of experience in high-level guard missions. They would be well armed, well equipped, and well-motivated. Kane knew that his team could not expect them to make mistakes.

"The Albanians want the nuclear schematics?" Brick said. "Are they trying to irradiate their sheep?"

Lord narrowed his eyes at Brick. "No, it wouldn't seem likely. But there is a high-level of corruption in the Albanian government. The Black Swan used Albania as one of his routes into Europe for his heroin."

Kane prickled at the mention of Naci. "Do we think they are on the Island? With Kohl?"

"In all likelihood," Lord affirmed. "But that intel is sketchy at best. We think, and some of our Agents in Tirana think the Albanians are trying to broker some deal between Naci and an as yet unknown player for the schematics."

"ISIS?" Kane leaned forward.

Lord shrugged. "What's left of them maybe. But either some state actor or terrorist faction can't be ruled out. But the mere fact the Albanians are putting this deal together suggests it's high level. And we're going to have to go in hard on White Skull."

"Oorah," breathed Brick. "This one is for the team members we lost."

Everyone in the room was sitting forward now. Kane got to his feet. "Thank you, Colonel. Reaper Team. We're up."

CHAPTER 18

Cutting across the waves, Reaper hugged the boat gunnels, leaning in low against the biting chill of the wind as it whipped up the chop and splashed ice across the bow as it slapped the surface. The Yamaha outboard motors purred, corkscrewing the propellers through the frigid salt water.

Kafka e Bardhë Island appeared, a black smudge on the black water against a midnight blue sky. Windswept, rocky, covered in grass and moss, it was a formidable location, unforgiving and austere. Kane scanned the craggy shoreline through a pair of powerful naval binoculars outfitted with ambient light intensification technology.

The dark, geometric shape of the old fish fishery emerged from the cold background, and he caught flickers of illumination too dim for normal vision. Someone was, indeed, on Kafka e Bardhë Island. And that someone was going to great lengths to hide their activity.

"Let's go say hello," he said, voice low.

"Approach?" Brick asked over the comm-link.

"Swing around to the south, where the cliffs rise out of the sea. The RENEA sentries will figure that for the least accessible ingress."

"We have to assume Kohl has given Naci a full briefing and that he knows our capabilities," Pop-Eye pointed out from just behind them, eschewing the comm to expand their radio silence.

"He's not telling a bunch of RENEA knuckle-draggers anything except that we're special operations. Out of all the approaches, going in the back door from the more arduously technical angle is still our best bet."

"Agreed." Hunt nodded.

A hundred yards out, Brick cut the engines and they rode the surf in.

Above them, the cliff loomed up out of the darkness, solid, indomitable. Pop-Eye moved forward in the boat and lifted a grapnel gun to his shoulder. The titanium hooks were coated in a sheath of industrial plastic to help muffle sounds. The tines came to sharp points.

The device coughed as the pneumatic ignition fired, and the nylon rope made a soft whirring sound as it played out up six stories over unforgiving boulders and past the rock lip. Hauling back on the line, Pop-Eye set the hook.

He looked over at Kane, who nodded. The SEAL stood and began climbing smoothly up the rope. Near the top, Pop-Eye paused, then slowly lifted his head past the edge, scanning the area for sentries. No one. He crawled over the cliff's lip and disappeared.

A moment later, he reappeared and waved the rest of the team up. One by one the team followed his lead, Brick coming last. The big man was the strongest individual on the team but, weighing the most and carrying the heaviest kit load, was the least agile on vertical ascent. Sliding over the top he found the rest of the team arrayed in a loose semi-circle, crouched and with weapons up.

The team fell into a Ranger file line with Pop-Eye at the front. Both the SEAL point man and Reaper verified compass readings and after a moment set out at a cautious pace. They were a little over a mile across the island from the abandoned fishing village.

A knife-edged wind pushed against them, cold even under their armor, and it pushed the wet grass against their legs as they moved. Through their Heads Up Display night vision, the landscape was a shifting tableau of cold grays, dull blues, and deep blacks. *Kafka e Bardhë* was a lonely, frigid rock thrusting out of the Adriatic.

Following natural contour lines, Team Reaper descended the hill and into an open area of sharply undulating topography. Cover was sparse, and Pop-Eye stopped frequently to scan ahead through the scope of his weapon. After twenty minutes of conservative hiking, they came out of a narrow defilade and settled among a clutch of boulders.

Below them at the bottom of a gentle slope leading down to the northeastern shore of the island, the dark and silent buildings of the village broke up the landscape. Little clapboard houses running along a small network of old streets spread out from the centralized structure of the fishery, which stood three stories high and ran roughly 150 yards long.

In a low voice, Pop-Eye said, "There's company."

————————

Spread out on all points of the compass, moving casually through the village, the green-white blurry silhouettes of the RENEA commandos stood out in vivid relief through the team's NVD optics. Directly below them, one of the Albanians stood with his back against a collapsed house, Kalashnikov assault rifle cradled in his arms.

"He's wearing night vision," Brick hissed.

"Yeah," Hunt agreed, "but those Albanian models gather and enhance ambient light. They work well, but they don't turn us into IR glow sticks."

"Pop-Eye," Reaper said.

The man lifted his weapon and lased his target. A green dot appeared on the Albanian, center mass. Pop-Eye exhaled and slowly let the dot drift up until it rested on the ridge of the RENEA trooper's nose, just below his mono-goggle. Pop-Eye's finger slowly tightened on his trigger.

thwack-thwack.

The sentry's head jerked, and he crumpled to the ground. As a unit, Team Reaper stood and began moving forward, spread out and covering different vectors of fire. In the lead, Pop-Eye abruptly froze. His hand came up in a fist. Immediately the team halted mid-stride.

A second RENEA trooper stepped out of the doorway of an abandoned building. Across the distance, on the breeze, they heard him asking a question through their helmet-integrated audio pickups. Pop-Eye lifted his weapon. The beam of the laser scope jumped across fifty yards and found the second Albanian.

Pop-Eye's weapon cycled through a three-round burst. The second sentry dropped to the ground next to the first, and the team continued their infiltration. Slipping up to the edge of the house, they stood guard while Brick and Rucker dragged the bodies out of the open and up against the foundation of the old building.

Wind chimes shivered on sagging porches, and the breeze whistled through cracks in the buildings. Windows stood broken out, and doors hung loosely on worn hinges. Small, unseen animals scurried through the wet grass and inside the rotting structures.

Crouched in the shadow of the house, Pop-Eye scanned both sides of the narrow avenue. Seeing nothing, he darted across and took up a position on the other side of the street. The rest followed. Three more times they repeated this process until they were deep inside the ghost town and near the water's edge.

Kane surveyed the fishery, casing the building like a burglar. He counted doors and windows, ran a practiced gaze over the uneven roof, and tried to ascertain which cluster of buildings near the large structure offered the best approach.

There was the crunch of feet on gravel.

Brick, holding rear security, turned in the direction of the sound. Up the street, a three-man squad of RENEA commandos in bulky body armor stepped around the corner of a building. The team remained still. They were just out of the Albanians' line of sight—on the ground, around the corner of a house. Their footsteps grew steadily louder as the three approached.

Pressed tightly against the building, the unit remained silent, their hearts beating steadily, as the RENEA sentries passed by, speaking quietly in Albanian among themselves. The smell of cigarette smoke floated after them.

Kane looked at Rucker, who nodded. Both men drew their silenced pistols and rose. Measuring each step, they stalked out into the street and fell in step behind the Albanians. The blunt ends of their sound suppressors rose in tandem.

Kane fired, dropped an Albanian, shifted his weapon, fired again, and dropped a second guard. Rucker's round entered his target at the junction of spine and skull where the hypothalamus hung in a grape-like cluster, regulating not only breathing but heartbeat. His bullet cored through the medulla oblongata and punched out the front of the man's throat.

As soon as the Albanians fell to the dirt road, Team Reaper was up and acting, retrieving the corpses and dragging them into the shadows against buildings. So far, fire discipline and a levelheaded approach had served them on the infiltration, but as they came closer to the target, they knew their skills—or luck—couldn't keep them unnoticed forever.

Reaper pointed to a line of dilapidated warehouses running from the water's edge to within mere feet of the concrete block fishery. "That's how we make our approach," he said. "We're going over the top and coming down on top of them."

"These roofs are shaky," Pop-Eye pointed out.

"That's why you're going first," Kane said. "If we

come to any areas you think won't support Brick, we'll reassess. But we got here on the fly, and General Thurston seems adamant that we're working against a ticking clock. Time is *not* a luxury we have."

There's no way I'm not getting these bastards today, Kane silently added.

Pop-Eye nodded and shrugged. The team slipped away, weaving in between houses, cutting across ancient overgrown lawns, and darting down narrow alleys until they reached the first of the old warehouses. The smell of the ocean was strong here; a line of rocky outcroppings protected the bay from the wind and allowed the water to collect in a calmer body.

An old wharf made of rotting timbers ran several meters out into the seawater, barnacle-encrusted pilings rising out of liquid that was black as oil. Across a wide flat parking lot, two Albanians walked with their backs to the team, headed toward massive sliding doors set above the fishery loading docks.

Pop-Eye looked over at Kane. Reaper shook his head.

"We don't want to leave anyone at our back," he said softly. "But we'd have to leave those two where they fell, out in the open. It's too great a risk. We'll deal with them once we're inside the building."

Rucker pointed into the mouth of the warehouse. "Look," he said. "There's a hole in the old ceiling from wind damage. We can get to the rooftops under cover instead of trying to scale from the outside. Once we're up, we can leapfrog from there to the fishery."

Kane nodded. "Let's do it, then, team."

Spreading out and moving in single-file line, the team slipped across the street and into the dark doorway leading into the old warehouse. Inside, an oil-stained concrete slab stretched away under the cavernous roof. A pile of old netting lay forgotten in a corner next to a pair of rusted metal buoys. Weather-damaged wooden pallets were stacked haphazardly around the area, forming indistinct towers in the pervasive gloom.

Pop-Eye turned and put his hand on Kane's shoulder. The SEAL pointed toward the large hole in the roof down low next to the rear wall. He leaned in close.

"Easy climb. I can jump, pull up, test the weight, and gauge our chances."

Reaper nodded. "Do it."

Pop-Eye let his weapon hang from the catches on his 3-point rifle sling. Flexing lightly at the knees, he leaped up, arms stretched out, and caught hold of the edge of the hole with his hands. He hung for a moment, testing to see if the board could hold his weight. Satisfied, he muscled himself easily up and disappeared through the opening.

Without needing to be told, Hunt used the Heads Up Display to initiate his electronic and digital recognition programs. Slowly he turned in a circle, walking a few steps in each direction. After a moment he turned back to Kane.

"I've got nothing close to us," he said.

Reaper nodded. "Let's be cautious as we move toward the fishery. Naci has all the money in the world to spend on intrusion-measures."

"Understood," Hunt said.

Behind them, Brick turned to ask Rucker a question—and discovered the man was gone. He looked around in surprise, momentarily confused as he tried to locate his teammate. After another moment, he spied the missing naval operator standing at the door to the warehouse, motionless.

An Albanian stepped through the doorway, ducking out of sight, and lit a cigarette, night-vision goggles pushed back atop his head like a kid with a ball cap. The lighter sparked twice then caught, illuminating the man's broad, soft-featured face in flickering, yellow light. Rucker materialized behind him.

The flame from the lighter reflected briefly in the American's helmet faceplate. The Albanian looked up at the last moment as if he sensed something, and Rucker unfolded like a snake striking. The lighter snapped off, and Brick watched the violent takedown through the green-tinged illumination of his enhanced optics.

Grabbing the Albanian by his broad forehead, Rucker snapped the soldier's neck back, exposing the big blood vessels of his throat and windpipe. *Snick.* The cold gray metal of Rucker's combat knife traced a line across the RENEA commando's throat. Blood rushed out over the man's uniform collar, absorbed by his shirt. The man's frantically-beating heart sent additional geysers spurting up in repeated arcs from the cleanly lacerated carotid artery.

The Albanian crumpled at the knees, and Rucker snatched the dead man's assault rifle out of his limp hands before it could clatter to the concrete. Brick moved forward to help him drag the body deeper inside.

"Next time, a heads up would be nice," Brick groused.

"But I want to keep the mystery in our relationship alive," Rucker said.

Kane hissed softly, catching their attention. He pointed upward toward the hole in the ceiling. "Let's go, gentlemen. We don't want to be late to the ball."

Rucker crossed over and leaped up, caught the edge, and pulled himself smoothly through the opening. A moment later, Brick and then Kane followed him. On the roof, they stayed low to avoid silhouetting themselves against the sky. Creeping forward they snuck quietly across the roof, almost to the fishery.

They passed by more sentries below.

RENEA were elite riot police, high-end security forces and close protection specialists. As such, their training focused less on long-range endurance and much more on hand-to-hand combat, crowd control techniques, and weight training.

Kane suspected Naci considered the unit perfect for a mission like this because they were used to deploying quickly in a protective role and being given little information as to the larger picture of the greater operational tasking.

Stand here. Guard this. Crack heads.

The federal police unit was a cut above regular military forces but was severely outclassed against a unit of Team Reaper's capability. Hugging the roofline, the Americans slipped past knots of the Albanian paramilitary police as they drew closer to their suspected target.

Halting on the roof of the building, they quietly lay prone. Below them, just to the opposite side of the main facility, they could see a small pier. Several rigid-hull, inflatable raiding craft were docked there. A lone RENEA sentry walked up and down beside the water, alert, but with his rifle slung over his shoulder.

Pop-Eye pointed at him and held his hands up, questioning. Kane shook his head. He leaned in closer to Pop-Eye and spoke quietly into the other man's ear.

"The boats might mean the submarine is outside the quay, probably on the bottom. There's zero reason for them to be ashore without Naci. Thurston was correct: Kohl is here."

"This might be the best chance we get," Hunt agreed. "We've caught up with them faster than they would expect if Kohl was aware we could trace him. They don't have access to fire support, reinforcements, or heavy weapons. RENEA is good but too used to beating people to death with clubs, not fighting somebody like us."

"A lot could go wrong," Reaper said. He paused. "More wrong than it already has," he corrected. "But we're in as good a place as we can expect. We take the building. Brick, we're going down the rabbit hole to make sure no one else gets in."

Brick lifted his machine-gun in one hand. "Not a problem."

Kane turned toward Pop-Eye. "Would you care to do the honors?"

"My pleasure."

Pop-Eye turned, lifted his carbine, lased the Albanian on the dock, and shot him. The man's legs buckled underneath him, and he fell, head bouncing on the unyielding ground. Pop-Eye turned back to Kane and gave him a thumbs up. "Five by five."

"Then let's do this," Reaper said.

Pop-Eye rose, testing the warehouse roof slightly before walking a short path, spot-checking the give on the building's materials. Satisfied, he slung his carbine and took three quick steps before clearing the distance between the building and the roof of the fishery.

At the zenith of his jump, he seemed to hang for a moment, suspended motionless, then he crossed the curve of his trajectory and shot out onto the fish-processing plant. Landing lightly after the short jump like a paratrooper coming in for a soft landing, he went down on a single knee. His weapon came up. Behind him, Rucker quickly followed Pop-Eye's example and jumped between the two buildings.

Landing, the SEAL rolled over on one shoulder and came up in a crouch. He was barely in position before Hunt landed beside him, weapon at the ready. They turned in opposite directions and took up ready positions.

Across from them, still on the first roof, Kane turned to Brick. "Stay sharp. Once we set this thing off, you should have targets converging on the double. Make them pay."

"Not a problem."

The big man pulled a protein bar from a Velcro pocket and tore it open with his teeth. Shoving the whole thing into his mouth, he began slowly masticating.

Kane slapped him on the shoulder and took the jump across the rooftop to land on the other side. As soon as he was ready, the team made for the second story where a line of old, broken windows overlooked their first-floor roof. As they crept forward, they became aware of a low undercurrent of buzzing coming through the ceiling of the old fishery.

Powerful machinery was at work inside.

Moving more speedily now, Reaper and the SEALs gathered around the salt silo. When the fishery had been in full operation, thousands of pounds of salt would be placed in the silo and added to the ground-up fish as part of the preparation process. A door in the roof opened out onto the squat cylinder, providing access for maintenance workers.

Pop-Eye reached over and tried the rusted doorknob. It turned under his hand—though a disquieting feeling stole over him when it did—and he gave Kane a quick nod. Noting the hinges to indicate which direction the door opened, Rucker took up a position on the edge of the door opposite the handle. The team tensed into their entry stack, ready to go in.

Rucker hesitated a moment. Something felt wrong. Bad, even.

Shrugging it off, he reached over and took a firm hold on the doorknob. He held up his free hand with three fingers out. He lifted and lowered his arm. Two fingers up. He lifted and lowered his arm. One finger. He lifted his arm a final time then lowered it. He quickly wrenched the door open in a single, smooth arc. Pop-Eye came out of his crouch, weapon up, and plunged through the doorway in a rush.

Hunt rose and sprinted toward the doorway, sensing something distressing in the air as he moved. Suddenly Pop-Eye came backpedaling out of the door and crashed into the lieutenant. Both men went down hard, tangled up in each other, weapons out of position and pinned between them.

Then came hell.

CHAPTER 19

Suddenly a stream of bullets whistled out of an opening.

"We've got company!" Pop-Eye shouted. More projectiles flooded the doorway, flying thick. The team rolled away from the fire. Pop-Eye blinked as an indeterminate number of figures emerged from the open doorway.

Pop-Eye started to call out, squinting to see what was in the middle of them. He shot at a diving RENEA uniform, but his bullets failed to connect with anything. He watched in powerless rage as an Albanian closed on Kane from behind. He impacted with Reaper from his blind spot, shoving him down again. He skittered dangerously close to the roof's edge.

Regaining his wits, Pop-Eye called out, "RENEA! Everyone scatter!"

The unit tried to spread out, too bunched together to fire all around without the risk of hitting each other. But the rooftop was extremely confined. Rucker swung away, trying for his sidearm when something smashed into his back, throwing him down. He dug his fingernails into the rooftop's irregular surface to keep from being thrown off.

Hunt turned from his frantic attempt to put some distance between himself and the Albanian. He assessed the scene that had developed on the rooftop.

A bullet smashed into Hunt's helmet, slamming the man to his knees.

Pop-Eye charged across the short expanse of roof and cautiously looked over the edge. He saw numerous RENEA unit closing in on the silo. He fired a burst of his P100 into the Albanians, forcing them to dive for cover.

"We got company close. You okay, Hunt?"

There was a moment's pause as the team waited, breath held, to see if the countermeasures specialist was going to recover. Hunt pushed himself up on shaky arms.

"That hurt," he said.

"Talk to me," Kane demanded over their audio pickups. "Quick reports. Keep it low—I don't know who's listening now."

"Some systems down," Hunt answered. He struggled to stand. "I'm not sure if I can still run all of my modules."

"Outer sentries are converging," Brick informed him. "Engaging."

The machine gun roared to life, immediately answered by half a dozen Kalashnikov rifles.

"I'm good," Pop-Eye said, but his voice was tight from pain. "Still, I'd like to not see that thing again, if everybody's okay with that."

"I can fight," Rucker said.

"Executive decision time," Kane announced. He shot a RENEA trooper firing from the broken-out window of an abandoned house two streets over. "We won't be coming back this way. No gauntlet home. We're taking those boats and getting out to open water where Cara can extract us. We'll have to reassess this mission from someplace a hell of a lot safer."

"Fire and maneuver, people," Hunt said, helping Pop-Eye to his feet.

"Fire in the hole," Rucker warned.

He lobbed a grenade into the open silo doorway as the rest of the unit began engaging the Albanian fighters. Red tracer fire cut in over their heads, brilliant as lasers in their image enhancers.

"We gotta get some cover," Kane said. He turned to Hunt. "We're sitting in a kill zone up here. Can you make the jump?"

Rucker's grenade went off, and black smoke poured out of the door.

"I can *fall* one story, if I have to," Hunt answered.

"I'm not that hurt."

"Fall one story, and then tell me that. Okay, down we go."

Hunt went down on his belly at the edge of the roof, slid over, and hung by his hands for a moment before dropping to the ground. He rolled like a paratrooper and came up, weapon unsteady but still ready. Above him bullets, burned into the roof. A round struck Kane in his breastplate, and he staggered backward but kept his balance.

Pop-Eye and Rucker backed across the open roof, weapons firing. Out in the abandoned village, they could see black-armored commandos scurrying to take up firing positions. Brick's machine-gun fire hammered into them with unforgiving force.

"You good?" Rucker shouted at Kane.

He waved him away. "Just get off the roof. I'm fine."

"Not this time, boss," the Special Forces medic told him. "I'll hold the line—you get down."

Kane didn't bother to argue; he was still fighting to catch his breath from the bullet's impact. More lead flew thick around them, forcing them onto their stomachs. Moving fast, Kane scooted backward off the roof and dropped.

"You next!" Rucker yelled at Pop-Eye.

"You go!"

"Screw you, you don't get to go first *and* last."

"Roger that," Pop-Eye said grudgingly. "Keep

your head down."

Pop-Eye rolled over the edge of the roof and dropped. Across the narrow gap between buildings, Brick let loose a long, ragged burst in the general direction of the enemy then immediately rolled over and followed the others down. Bullets struck the roof around Rucker. A round struck his weapon and snapped it out of his hands. The sling tangled around his head for a moment, blinding him, and he pulled it up and away from his face, casting it aside. But he couldn't see where it went—blinding tracers cut the air inches above his head.

He twisted in what felt like a firing squad, momentarily losing his balance, and he fell hard, backward off the roof. Slamming down to the ground, he lay stunned for a moment. Brick crossed the little alley to him and leaned in to haul him to his feet. Rucker sat up slowly, drawing his pistol as he did. He caught movement out of the corner of his eye and turned. A RENEA trooper stood in a window, AKS up.

Kane fired from behind them, and the Albanian's face disappeared in a cloud of red vapor. Hunt threw a smoke grenade into the alley, and Pop-Eye followed suit. In seconds, a dense wall of gray-white smoke screened them from their enemies.

A big Albanian, carrying himself with alarming disinterest in his own safety, appeared out of the smoke. Though dressed only in Albanian fatigues, he held an RPK machine-gun up and ready in both hands.

Reaper shot at him, and the figure rolled back into the smoke. It was unclear if Kane's shot had hit him or not.

"We don't want to be here if he gets up," the team leader muttered to no one.

Still half-carrying Rucker, Brick turned and ran for the dock. The medic regained his equilibrium after a few steps and began running on his own. Hunt dived in and started a motor on one of the launches; the unit slid into the rigid hull inflatable boat. Brick tossed a third smoke grenade as Pop-Eye used his big hunting knife to slice through the moorings.

They were out of the dock in less than a minute.

The launch headed into the bay, turning for open water. Kane quickly switched over his transmission frequency. "Cara, you have me?"

"You're up, good signal," Cara said.

"Fragmentation order. We're coming out hot from the north-side approach. Repeat, north-side approach."

"You had me at hot, Julio."

Kane didn't bother to answer. Scimitar cut the boat away from shore just as the big Albanian and his machine-gun appeared on the dock. Brick fired at him, and the Spetsnaz went to his stomach and opened up with the RPK. His burst slapped into the water short of the team.

RENEA officers emerged from the smoke, reaching the edge of the water. As a unit Team Reaper opened up, putting out a wall of lead as they sped away, Hunt gunning the throttle until it ran wide open. The boat tore across the water, cascading up the waves and slamming back down hard. The impact rattled them all, throwing off their aim and threatening to toss them clear.

Hunt cut sharply to the side to confuse the Albanian fire. A round struck one of the twin outboards and it immediately began to sputter. Their speed dropped as half their horsepower rapidly disappeared. Two hundred yards out, Hunt compensated by cutting another hard angle and running out to the east, using the topography of the island to blunt some of the small-arms fire.

He looked around as the team began pulling themselves out of the bottom of the boat.

"They sort of kicked our asses," Pop-Eye pointed out.

Kane looked down as his communication channel lit up. "I'm here."

"Newsflash," Cara said in his headset, "they evacuated the target. I told you not to ring the doorbell."

"You have eyes on them?"

"Negative. I'm coming to pick up your sorry asses."

Kane hesitated. He looked at the others. Rucker nodded as if he understood Kane's hesitation.

"If we're going back," he offered, "we're going to need bigger guns."

"That's why we have a helicopter," Kane replied, "so we don't have to go back this time. We'll be utilizing Plan B."

"Copy. Prepare for incoming."

"Light them up." Kane signed off. He saw the look in their eyes—Reaper Team knew why they weren't returning to the island to find Kohl and the Black Swan. They knew, by the order he'd just given, that Kohl had escaped.

On the other end of the frequency, the pilot reached over and snapped up a red switch, revealing a toggle. He clicked it over. Beneath the craft, a missile platform dropped down on two hydraulic arms. Satellite-guided Enhanced Patriots fired, afterburners exploding to life.

The missiles leaped out of their tubes and dropped down just off the dock. Guidance fins snapped out, and the weapon system ran in a straight course back toward the island. Flying fast, the missiles soared overhead, passing a collision course to the island.

"Knock, knock," Pop-Eye said, watching them go. "Candygram."

"That shit's gluten free and everything," Brick snorted. But there wasn't any real humor in it; all they could do in the aftermath of the failed mission was watch the fireworks.

It wasn't disappointing.

"I guess we know what happens now," Hunt said. "The after-action report to Colonel Lord on this engagement is not going to be flattering."

"You're a real killjoy," Pop-Eye told him.

"Not really. We don't have anything to be joyous about in the first place," he replied.

No other bothered to argue.

CHAPTER 20

And indeed, Colonel Lord was not happy. Kane spent the next 24 hours at Bagram when they'd returned, filling in the new asshole he'd had ripped, with coffee.

"You went in too hot and you know it."

"Sir."

"The trail is cold. Right now, we don't have them anywhere. Perhaps an Albanian navy submersible got them away. Or something else. You will keep Reaper at mission ready status. You will be here in this briefing room at three seconds' notice as soon as we have a lead to go on. Is that clear?"

"Crystal, sir."

"Keep polishing that crystal, Kane. I don't want to stand on your neck like this again. But I will."

The Tirana lead came in thirty-six hours later.

They were already on a C-130 from Bagram to Aviano Air Base at the foot of the Carnic Alps in Northern Italy before all plans for the raid had been finalized.

Abdul Manani, Naci's paymaster had been zeroed by agents in the city. He was in town, so the chatter said, setting up a meeting to discuss the sale of the schematics with person unconfirmed as yet. But the Organized Crime and Triad Bureau (OCTB) out of Hong Kong, had already let Interpol know, and through them Langley, that two operatives from the Tai Huen Chai—The Big Circle Boys—one of the largest Triads in Hong Kong had travelled to Tirana at the same time.

"Nuclear Centrifuge schematics might not be of ultimate interest to a Triad known mainly for people and drug smuggling, but if Naci was looking to ingratiate himself with the Triads, convince them he was a bigger player by selling them something that they could then sell on for even greater influence and power, then sending Manani in to set up a deal made sense." Kane was briefing on the C-130. Reaper Team were checking gear and getting Mission Hot.

Nënë Tereza, the international airport serving Tirana, Albania was to be their target. Not knowing how deep the Albanian government or its officials were into this, meant they were going in dark. They would fly from Aviano, at daisy cutter height across the Adriatic, inland to the airport and hit the building where Manani had been zeroed—a nondescript office building in the airport grounds where the meeting was supposed to take place, according to Interpol.

They would recover Manani, and the schematics, and if they took out a couple of Hong Kong lowlifes along the way then so be it. "The Albanians might wail in the UN once the mission was over," Colonel Lord said. "But let them. If they weren't facilitating business like this, then we'd be happy to cooperate. Once you have the schematics."

Within an hour of landing at Aviano, with Reaper Team in the air, they would refuel on the USS Ingraham from Destroyer Squadron 60, of the United States Navy Sixth Fleet, in the Adriatic, and launch the mission from there, flying under radar at combat height and speed.

"We need to be in and out of there slicker than a mouthful of snot," Kane said. "Operation Swiftest Arrow."

"Operation International Incident," said Brick.

Kane thumped him on the helmet and grinned.

"Just do the thing."

"I am the thing," Brick replied.

Things didn't much go south, as fall off the map while swallowing the compass.

They came through the door fast. Pop-Eye

peeled left, hugging the wall, coming up almost immediately against another wall and following that down. Behind him, Kane entered and moved to the right, also running along the wall. He confronted a figure staggering in the smoke, hands held up to its ears, utterly oblivious and stunned by the explosion.

Kane put a three-round burst center mass, and gore splattered the wall as the figure spun and dropped.

Hunt entered third with his weapon, a Saiga-12 fully automatic shotgun with drum magazine the M501, to cover the center space. He swept the weapon in a tight clearing motion and then sidestepped to the left as Brick made his entry with his M62.

The room was an unremarkable-looking office with a receptionist desk and waiting room chairs. The breached door lay in smoldering, twisted metal strips, and a coffee table sat cracked apart by the entry blast. A potted bamboo plant stand was shattered, scattering stalks and potting soil across the thin carpet. The room smelled like smoke and searing lead.

A door stood to one side of the office desk, and it led deeper into the building. Kane nodded at Rucker. The medic shuffled forward. His entire drum magazine was filled with breaching rounds. The modified shotgun shells were useful not only for blowing out locks or hinges, but the powdered metal loads also made effective anti-personnel rounds.

He triggered a double burst from the Saiga M501, and two fist-sized holes bored through the door, tearing the knob and locking mechanism apart. Pop-Eye stepped forward and kicked the broken remnants of the door inward.

Again, the team moved in choreographed, almost mechanical, unison. Weapons up, vectors covered, they entered the corridor. Outside, the Little Bird hovered as the team pushed deeper into the building.

Speed. Surprise. Violence of action.

Overhead, industrial-style track lighting gleamed harshly off linoleum floors. Reaper and his cohorts moved quickly but carefully, running the penetration by the numbers. They did not race toward their possible death with blind, frantic speed. Slow was smooth. Smooth was fast.

Coming to a door, Brick knelt on the hard plastic and rubber of his armored kneepad with his light machine gun at the ready as he covered the team's rear security. The other four members of the unit entered the room and cleared it.

They heard angry voices shouting in Albanian deeper inside the Ministry building. More agents were responding to the attack. Even though the offices were a twenty-four-hour operation, their cover called for the appearance of normal business hours, meaning the team now dealt with a reduced staff.

Unfortunately, a higher percentage of that reduced staff was highly trained security personnel. They were all well-armed, so Reaper's team could not afford to leave unchecked any door or room at their backs, despite the intensely tight operational timeline.

Three times they repeated the pattern, clearing offices and then a conference room. At the fourth door, they found the entrance to the stairwell just as a security team burst into the corridor from the opposite end.

The Albanian security team was enmeshed in black Kevlar helmets and riot gear. Each soldier in the six-man squad held a Type-79 submachine gun—except for the man running point, who wielded a compact QSV-92 9mm pistol he fired immediately from around a full-length ballistic riot shield.

The hallway exploded.

Pop-Eye reacted instantly, triggering a three-round burst from his P100 as Brick threw himself down to the ground on his belly and cut loose with the M62, laying down waves of suppressive fire.

Kane yanked open the door and shoved Rucker inside. Hoping for psychological effect as much as kill shots, Scimitar unleashed a long burst from the

Saiga M501, and the 12-gauge rounds pounded out a deafening tempo in the confined space.

Kane grabbed the medic by the shoulder and shoved Hunt through the door after Rucker. A bullet punched through the interior door and struck the unit leader high in the chest. Kane grunted under the impact as his body armor absorbed the slug.

Pop-Eye hit Kane with a shoulder block, shoving him through the door, and fired his P100 with one hand. On the floor, Brick coolly sent walls of lead toward the Albanian team as the security personnel returned fire around their shield man.

Gasping from the impact, Kane snapped, "Help cover!"

"On it," Rucker replied.

He already held a grenade in his hand. Yanking out the pin on the M67 anti-personnel grenade, he hooked it around the corner through the door with a hard snap of his arm, letting the arming spoon spring free.

Immediately Brick cut off his cover fire and rolled through the doorway. Two seconds later, the grenade went off. Like a sound tunnel, the hallway projected the ear-splitting effect of the explosion.

"Those seem like regular guards for a low-key facility like this to you?" Scimitar demanded.

"Hell no," Rucker answered. "Those boys were already suited up for trouble. That was the courier escort team."

"Go," Kane ordered. "Up the stairs. We need the high ground." He reached up to his throat-jack and engaged his communications. "Cara, this is Reaper."

"Go ahead, Reaper," Cara replied.

"Primary contact established," he said. "Be ready for runners. Increase altitude."

"Copy that," the pilot answered, "but this means the clock is ticking."

Cara cut in with, "If you want your ride out of there not to go down in a ball of flame, you better shake what your mama gave ya."

"Roger. Reaper out." Kane looked at the team. "You heard the lady. Let's roll."

CHAPTER 21

Snapping his P100 into position, Pop-Eye started up the stairs, muzzle up. It was a typical office building fire-access staircase, running in a squared spiral with a new landing at each level. The point man reached and cleared the second-story entry point in seconds.

Five hundred yards away, the traffic was still going along the road outside the airport, headlights slicing the night and a Boeing 757 was making final approach.

The team followed Kane up the stairs, quickly forming a tight defensive knot. Again, Pop-Eye's weapon was orientated upward while Hunt used the assault shotgun to cover the fire door that led to the second story. Crouched in the middle, Kane expertly coordinated the team.

Slapping Brick on one big shoulder, Kane nodded. The man leveled the M62 and sent rounds pouring down the stairwell and into the first-floor doorway to discourage anyone from following too closely. Kane turned toward Rucker. The hollow-eyed man looked back through the visor on his helmet. His eyes were inscrutable. Kane leaned in close.

"It's time," he told his XO. "See if you can find the device."

Rucker nodded and turned to begin.

Four rounds slammed through the door at head height. Hunt, firing from one knee, sent three breaching rounds in a diagonal pattern back through the door. "Pistol rounds, single shooter," he announced.

"Keep his head down, let Rucker work," Kane demanded.

"Aye, aye, Captain Bligh," Hunt answered.

Triggering four more rounds through the doorway, he narrowed his focus. Each load of powdered metal seared through the structure material, leaving holes the size of coffee cups, even from that extended range. The door sagged inward on its frame.

From his position, Pop-Eye's carbine erupted in chain bursts as he fired up the stairs. In response, a flurry of rounds hammered back into the first-level door. Brick fired a long figure-eight pattern in return.

"Magazine!" he yelled.

Instantly Kane pivoted and began firing over Brick's head. The big man swapped out compact ammo compartments for the caseless rounds of his M62 with quick, economic motions.

Above them, Pop-Eye used his trigger finger to drop the thirty-round magazine out of his own weapon as his other hand brought a fresh one up, securing it in the well. He tapped the catch release, and the bolt slid home with a greasy *snap*. He was good to go.

He triggered another three-round burst.

Despite his suppressive fire, incoming RENEA rounds pinged off the walls, leaving scorch marks or digging out furrows, ricocheting off metal handrails and hammering into steps. The team's ballistic armor began taking blunt force strikes, absorbing deadly kinetic energy from the rounds but leaving the operatives increasingly bruised and battered.

Kane shifted his stuttering carbine to a single grip and returned the grasp. The men locked hands. Through their gloves, their palms ran slick with sweat as Reaper tried in vain to take some of the agony off Rucker, to absorb some of it himself.

Rucker contorted, his chest hammering against his ribs. His head snapped to first one side and then the other. Suddenly, his grip fell slack in Kane's hand.

"Up," he gasped. "The sonuvabitch is up."

"You heard the man," Kane said. "Up. Move, damn it."

Hunt fired two more bursts into the second-floor door and rose, sidestepping up the stairs. Kane pushed a weakened Rucker up the stairwell after Pop-Eye and Hunt. Behind them, Brick rose from his belly into a crouch, triggering the M62 one-handed as he freed a grenade from his web gear.

He brought the explosive next to the pistol grip of his light machine gun and slid the metal loop pin around that thumb. Yanking it free, he peeled off and let the spoon bounce down the steps. With a single hook-shot motion, he snapped the M67 explosive device down the staircase toward the first floor and spun around to charge up the steps after his team.

On the move, he shifted his muzzle upward and added his own volume of suppressive fire to that of the others. Their unit was attempting to outgun their way clear of a strategically weaker position. Rucker stumbled unsteadily on his feet, and Kane kept one arm tucked under the man's shoulder as the lieutenant fought to compose himself.

The grenade went off below them. Kane got on his throat-mic. "Light up One and Two, Air support," he told her. "I say again: One and Two."

"Copy, Reaper."

Outside the building, the pilot let the Blackhawk drift slightly as Cara shifted the muzzle apparatus of the M134 minigun into position. Grinning, they made it rain lead. In a hot flash, a storm of 7.62mm NATO rounds slammed into the building, chewing apart the walls and blasting out windows.

Lighting up the building they put 100 rounds straight through the blown-out front door and punched slugs across the reception area and down into the hallway. The second half of the Albanian defense team, waiting to attempt entry, was ripped apart.

"Third floor?" Kane demanded.

Rucker nodded. "I'm positive."

"Good. Disengage module. We'll do the rest of this the old-fashioned way."

The gunmen ambushing them from above were driven back as Reaper and his team charged the stairs in assault mode. Halfway up to the third-floor landing, both Pop-Eye and Kane triggered HE rounds from their under-slung 30mm grenade launchers.

The projectiles slammed into the fire door, blowing it off the hinges and cramming the doorjamb straight back out of the frame. Black smoke billowed. Collateral damage was not a concern, and Pop-Eye performed reconnaissance by fire as he advanced, blindly placing bursts of the blended metal APLP rounds through the door.

They came through the doorway, splitting apart to cover both directions. A man in a business suit lay torn in half on the carpet, his entrails strung out like party streamers across the floor.

For a moment, everything was still except for the drifting smoke and the sound of the gunship's minigun raining hellfire down on the building below them.

"Which way?" Pop-Eye demanded.

Rucker, still recovering, pointed down the hall to the left. "That way," he said. "One of those three doors."

"By the numbers, Reaper," Kane told them. "Give me medical and ammunition reports."

Each man quickly disavowed anything beyond bruises. The combat load for this smash and grab called for a basic template. To a man, they were down around the fifty percent mark on ammunition.

Once again, the team folded into its stack and began advancing. Hunt took advantage of the opportunity provided by the momentary lull to drop out his partially spent ammo drum and replace it with a full one. He clicked it into place and covered the team's six while Brick changed out his own magazine.

The stack tightened up, and Pop-Eye led them down the hall. Coming to the first door, he went down on a knee. Carefully, he reached across the door and tried the knob. It was unlocked.

Slowly, he twisted the handle.

7.62mm Tokarev rounds punched through the interior walls. Pop-Eye took rounds in his body armor at his shoulder, triceps, and waist. The kinetic energy spun him around and laid him flat out on the ground, stunned. His carbine dropped out of his hand and clattered to the floor.

As one, the team threw themselves off the wall, leveling their weapons. Hunt walked three breaching rounds down the line of exposed hinges on the door. His ceramic breastplate cracked as he was struck center mass through the door. He staggered backward, triggering a 12-gauge round into the floor, as the wind sledgehammered his lungs with the impact.

Brick cut loose with everything the M62 could give him, driving a long, ragged burst through the wall and into the room beyond. Kane kicked the hinge-less door out of the way and fired through it. He stutter-stepped in, cut left along the wall, hunting for targets.

Right behind, Rucker followed him in, firing then peeling off to the right. Hunt pushed himself off the far wall, braced the Saiga, and came through the door firing shotgun shells in the systemic cadence of a pitching machine launching baseballs.

In the hallway, Brick knelt next to the stunned Pop-Eye and covered the hallway with his light machine gun. Sucking in air to fill his lungs, Pop-Eye tried feeding his oxygen-starved muscles after the adrenaline-fueled exertion. With each breath came the stink of death and the overpowering scent of weapons fire.

"You good?" he asked Pop-Eye, who was still gasping.

"Yeah," the point man managed. "I've got a bitchin' pain in my ribs, but I don't think I'm too injured." He paused. "Not too much."

"We'll get a stim-shot. Have you pepped right up. We're almost out of here. I mean, after that, what else could go wrong, right?"

"Reaper," the pilot cut in. "I have RENEA on the roof engaging me and Tirana police units responding from the main terminal."

"Copy," Kane answered from inside the room. "We'll extract the package and will be on your twenty momentarily."

Just down the hall, a door swung open and a riot-armored figure pointed a Type-79 submachine gun at Brick. Both men triggered their weapons simultaneously. Angry metal hornets of 7.62mm Tokarev rounds buzzed toward the team's machine gunner as he fired his own burst of 6.8mm caseless slugs.

Brick took a round in the top of his helmet that snapped his head back.

A second round skidded across his visor at an angle, cracking it and driving plastic splinters into his face. He sprawled backward, finger still on the trigger. The muzzle flash of his weapon lit up, and the weapon bucked wildly in his grip.

Two rounds slammed into his chest, knocking him back. From the floor, Pop-Eye aimed his P100 and killed the enemy soldier with a tight, accurate grouping.

Inside the room Hunt, Rucker, and Kane surveyed the wreckage of the battle.

Directly behind the door, a riot-geared combatant was sprawled out on the floor. His submachine gun lay blown into separate pieces and his armor hung off his frame, cracked from close-in bullet impacts.

A female police officer in the blue uniform of the Albanian Police lay draped along the edge of a heavy conference room table. She'd taken a breach round to the head and several dozen high-velocity rounds to the body.

A man lay on the floor, grotesquely mutilated; however, his uniform did not match the woman's. His was olive green, the color of the Albanian military law enforcement agency.

Hunt walked over and looked down at the man.

"He's RENEA," Rucker said. "That means those boys in the riot gear are either from the Immediate Action Unit or Federal Police," he said, referencing two of the organization's elite paramilitary forces. "We're going toe-to-toe with their heavy hitters."

"Good news is," Hunt said, "we won't need a key or hacksaw."

A third body, that Kane immediately recognized as what was left, well about two thirds say, of the Paymaster. He'd taken the blast full on and it had dismantled him torso from limbs. His face had the frozen look of shock of those that had been instantly killed. One eye was popped out almost on his cheek, and it would be the work of a moment to say hello to his brains.

There was an attaché case attached to Manani's wrist by a chain. Fortunately for Hunt, who was bending down to look at it, the arm was no longer connected to Manani's shoulder. The dead RENEA operatives again gave credence that this was an officially sanctioned Albanian operation.

There was something very rotten in the state of this particular Denmark.

Scimitar picked up the blood-smeared attaché case. Tethered to the case was a long chain that led to steel handcuffs on the man's wrist. The man's arm was blown off at the elbow. Chief Borden turned toward Rucker, holding out the gory prize like a trophy.

"Is it inside?"

Rucker took the case in his hands, ignoring the dangling, dripping limb. He concentrated for a moment; his expression impossible to read behind the face shield of his helmet. After a moment, he nodded.

CHAPTER 22

"That's it. Let's go. We'll let the EOD boys open it in case our Albanian friends decided to put fail-safes in place."

"Agreed," Kane said.

Outside the room, gunfire exploded in another sudden, violent exchange. The pilot's voice broke over the ear-jack inside their helmets.

"People, these vehicles responding are more RENEA units, not Security police. They're going to have heavier artillery. May I suggest we've over-stayed our welcome?"

"Copy," Kane answered. He lifted his weapon, heading toward the room door to cover Pop-Eye and Brick. "We're in route to exfil, over."

As they began to move, a grenade went off.

———

Kane threw himself against the ruined doorjamb and cut loose with stuttering bursts from his weapon. He saw Brick and Pop-Eye lying motionless on the hallway floor, faces down, weapons wildly cast aside, limbs limp.

"Men down, Medic!" he shouted. "Rucker!"

Rucker didn't need further direction. As Kane poured fire down the hall from his position against the far-side doorjamb, Hunt slid into position on his knees. He popped open the slide on the AGS 30mm grenade launcher that was attached below the barrel of his weapon and slid another HE round into the breech.

"You ready?" he asked Hunt. His voice was calm.

He nodded.

"Do it."

Popping low around the door, Hunt triggered the AGS. Its distinctive *bloop* sound was clearly audible over the persistent staccato of Kane's covering fire. Because of the safety mechanism involving the arming device, Hunt put his round into the wall a few meters down from the doorway they received fire from.

The wall crumpled inward like the sides of a beer can, and the concussive force of the explosion cracked in a shockwave down the funnel of hallway. Flames ignited as building materials caught fire, and smoke from the high-explosive round filled the narrow corridor.

Moving instantly, Rucker snatched his fallen teammates up by the collars and with great effort hauled them back into the room. Panting heavily, he performed a rapid trauma assessment first on Pop-Eye and then on Brick. Already, Pop-Eye was rousing. Brick's face was a mass of blood, but his wounds seemed superficial. They both breathed on their own, and neither showed major bleeding. Still, there was no way to assess what kind of injuries might be under their respective armor.

Rucker looked at Kane. "Stim-shot and make for the backdoor. That's my professional medical opinion."

"Four out of five dentists agree," Pop-Eye spoke up, his voice thick from his pain. "Come on, Doc, good stuff."

"No Special K 'til we're in the Blackhawk," Rucker said. "You be a good boy and kill everything between here and there, and I'll hit you on the ride back in."

"Where's my weapon?" Pop-Eye asked.

"Atta-boy."

"Shortest distance between two lines is a straight point," Rucker said.

"What the hell does that mean?" Kane asked.

"It means we're taking fire from the hall. We've got two men slowed."

"I'm fine!" Brick argued, coming around after Rucker's stim-shot.

"Shut up," Rucker said. His voice was as close to pleasant as it got.

"Go on," Kane said.

"The gunship has driven the security element on the roof back down into the stairs. This is starting to shape up like the last ten minutes of Butch Cassidy and the Sundance Kid."

"We've been here before," Pop-Eye pointed out.

"Yeah, but we were inside CONUS," Rucker replied, using the military shorthand for Continental United States. "We got out of the hard spot there, but we didn't have an entire military gearing up to block us clocking out."

"You were saying something about straight lines?" Kane prompted.

Rucker nodded. He pointed at the floor of the room. "Point A," he said. He pointed at the ceiling. "Point B."

Kane stepped forward, nodding. "Rucker keeps the Bull cooking. Hunt lays down a crossfire here. It'll work but not for long. You guys need to shake your asses."

"That's not a problem," Pop-Eye said. "Shaking his ass is how Rucker got through college."

Brick nodded, his face earnest behind the mask of blood and the halo of his shattered face shield. "No, that's true."

"Secure the door," Kane told them. "Rucker, help me get this conference table into position. Pop-Eye, do your thing."

The point man already had his backpack off and open. He pulled clear an E-Z Breach Entry Port model shape charge. The heavy explosive module was specifically designed to blow holes large enough to permit personnel egress through walls, all just using a water tamp charge bladder.

"Gunship, this is Reaper," Kane said into his throat-mic.

"Reaper," the pilot answered immediately, "I am reading status critical on my ammunition. I've kept law enforcement response vehicles at a good stand-off perimeter, but more are rolling in. We don't have long until air assets reach our AO."

"Understood. The personnel on the roof, are there any left?"

"Negative. The ones that weren't KIA re-entered the building."

"Copy. Give the roof a safety zone. We're breaching. You deploy the SPI/E through our improvised egress point."

"Reaper, did I copy 'improvised egress point,' over?"

"Copy."

"I assume there will be no doubt as to your twenty when this happens, over?"

Kane looked over at Pop-Eye. The point man smiled back and pulled a second water breach shape charge from his backpack.

"Gunship, there will be no doubt," he told them.

"Copy," she paused.

"Time is of the essence," the pilot added.

"Just be ready to drop the line," he answered.

"Gunship out."

Kane and Rucker kicked the bodies clear of the bullet-riddled conference table as Pop-Eye prepped the charges, first by ripping the covers off the adhesive strips and then by attaching detonators into the thick, clay-like blocks of plastic explosive.

At the doorway, Rucker and Brick formed X-pattern fields of overlapping cover fire from the ruined jamb. As Pop-Eye climbed up onto the table, Kane unhooked a pale green grenade, roughly the shape of a soda can, from his web gear suspender.

"Rucker," he called. The medic ceased firing and looked back. Kane tossed the grenade to him in an easy underhand pitch. Rucker caught it with one hand. "Start a fire," he told the naval medic. "Couldn't hurt to slow 'em down."

Rucker nodded and yanked the pin free from the Model 308-1 Napalm grenade. He tossed the incendiary device underhand through the door, where it bounced off a wall, struck the floor, and rolled down the hall toward the staircase, where the survivors of the paramilitary team from the roof had attempted their entry into the hallway.

Prior to the operation, Kane had added gasoline to the M1 powdered napalm "thickener", creating

Hell-in-a-Can. The resulting flash immediately set the corridor ablaze.

"*Now* we're cooking with gas," Hunt muttered.

He lifted his drum-fed assault shotgun and triggered a long automatic blast through the quickly rising flames, just to remind the enemy there was still a gunslinger and hell-hammer operating behind the thick wall of smoke.

Pop-Eye slapped both of the breaching charges to the ceiling using their adhesive strips, and he hopped down. The water bladder attached to the back of the plastic explosive was all the resistance the explosive needed to direct the blast straight up into the ceiling at the moment of detonation.

He helped Rucker and Kane dump the table onto its end so it could be placed up against the charges, wedging them further into place. Long wire cords snaked down, and he quickly wrapped them together, exposed the inner laces, and twisted them into a single length before inserting them into the detonator.

"Cover up!" he ordered.

The team placed themselves in corners, curling up with the protection of their body armor and equipment packs.

Rucker turned his helmeted head toward Kane. "I suppose there's a chance the whole roof could come down." It wasn't a question.

"The helicopter took enough gun runs at this

building. I wouldn't be surprised if the whole structure collapsed."

"Excellent. Leadership by optimism. I like it."

"Thought I'd try it on for size."

"Fire in the hole!" Pop-Eye yelled.

The blast ripped through the ceiling, and smoke billowed back in fast rushing clouds, obscuring vision in a sudden wall of fog. The shape charge punched up through the ceiling with irreconcilable force, spewing table-size chunks of construction materials into the air like confetti.

Overhead, they heard the thumping sound of rotor blades as the pilot brought the helicopter into a tight hover. A long, thick rope with loops of canvas sewed into it uncoiled as it fell and hit the splinter-covered floor of the office. The team moved quickly, securing themselves to the rope by the D-ring climbing carabiners at hard points on their body armor.

The technique was known as "SPIE" or SPI/E— Special Patrol Infiltration/Extraction—and it was a common operational tool for reconnaissance troops and special operations forces. Kane clicked himself into place. He held the severed arm attached to the briefcase by the bloody stump of its elbow.

First Pop-Eye, then Rucker, Brick, and Hunt signaled him with thumbs up. The three men prepped final hand grenades as Kane talked to the pilot.

"Reaper on, let's go!"

"About time. It's been almost eight minutes on-site," the pilot answered. "Our maritime element is screaming my ear-jack off."

The helicopter's power plant howled as it lifted straight up and cleared the building. Below them, the three hand grenades went off in a daisy chain string of explosions. All five men readied the next round of grenades.

At altitude, the warehouse district below the main runways was laid out like a game board. Its avenues and alleys swarmed with uniformed figures, official vehicles, and wailing sirens. Two sedans sat, perforated as cheese graters, while one vehicle was fully engulfed in flame. A pair of twisted and torn bodies lay sprawled in pools of what, from Reaper's height, looked like oil.

The pilot lifted the tail rotor and pointed the helicopter's nose toward the sea for its final run across open water as the five men released their ordnance. The smoke grenades, already leaking gray tails, fell fast, spreading quickly to obscure vision and increase confusion.

Rucker's dry voice came over the net. "Well, if the boys behind the desks wanted to send Albanian drug lords a message, I'd say it was delivered."

"Yeah, I'd say so," Kane answered. There wasn't a trace of irony in his voice; it was simply a tired acknowledgment. "And we're just the boys for this kind of delivery."

CHAPTER 23

Kane blinked sweat from his eyes as the heat of the western-Afghanistan afternoon blasted through the open door of the red Toyota Landcruiser. Hands pulled at his shirt as he was yanked from the vehicle and thumped down onto the ground.

The dust was already in his mouth and stuck to the sweat on his face as two vicious kicks hit him in the kidneys, and he was squashed down into the dirt to smear more of the gritty soil on his face. His shoulders ached where his wrists were zip tied behind his back, and his knees were sore from where he'd already been held in a stress position for two hours, before Midnight had made the negotiations with Naci to bring the Reaper Team leader in to the compound where this whole shitty episode in Kane's life had begun.

He noticed as the female mercenary had driven into the compound that nothing remained of the battle that had set the first dominoes in this shit show tumbling—back when Team Reaper hadn't been a dwindling unit of brothers and sisters caught up in one failed mission after another.

Guards from the compound had met them fifteen miles away and checked both Midnight and Kane over for trade materials or surveillance devices, trackers or weapons. Only Midnight had a gun, a black bladed stiletto knife and a SIG Sauer.

She had not been allowed to keep the knife or the gun. The guards were not taking any chances with them.

They had given Kane a beating just for shits and giggles before bundling him back into the Landcruiser and riding with them for the rest of the way.

Now they gave Kane another couple of kicks, laughing at him in the dirt, and then picked him up to drag him inside the building.

Inside it stank of cooking. The floor was no less dusty than the yard outside. There were rugs across what looked like bare dirt floors, and the walls had an unfinished look about them. It was as if they knew there was no point finishing the place—it wouldn't be needed for that long.

The only sop of comfort Kane could see as he was dumped onto a complicated and knotted Afghan rug were three expensive looking leather sofas. There was a workstation with six screens showing all angles of approaches to the compound, a young man in brown robes who was trying to grow a beard cycled through the images. Making notes on a pad next to the keyboard.

There was a large TV hanging from the wall on the opposite end of the room. It was silent, but the picture was showing a European soccer game being played a quarter of a world away. Players danced and skipped over the turf, close ups of the crowd cheering seemed to be cheering at Kane's plight as he lay there trying to get his breath back after the beating and the kicking.

Midnight arranged herself on the sofa like a spider contemplating its next meal and the guards took up positions either side of Kane. Only one eye was far enough above the rug to see anything else, so it was a disembodied voice that came to him next. But it was one he recognized from a particularly tense meeting in Zehedan.

"Gunnery Sergeant Kane. How nice of you to drop in," said Kohl.

Whether he was keeping out of Kane's eyeline deliberately or not, the voice stayed disembodied.

"Welcome to the—well for the moment—Naci residence. We're not planning on being here much longer, but how could we pass up the opportunity to meet with you one last time?"

"Don't mind me," said Kane. "I'm happy just to have a nap here and you can send me a postcard. Where from? Hong Kong? Tirana? Syria?"

Kohl's laughter hissed like the cobra Kane had killed outside the ex-station deputy's secret residence. Perhaps they were related...

"I don't think you're in any position to make smart ass comments Gunnery Sergeant. Midnight has brought you here to be killed, and that's what we're going to do. But there will need to be some interrogation first."

"I won't tell you anything. You know that."

"Of course, you won't. I didn't say we wanted to interrogate you for information, I just want to interrogate you—for fun."

"Every man should have a hobby."

"Turn him over."

One of the guards rolled Kane onto his back with his boot. The ceiling was as rough as the walls, and black power cables ran in lines across it, hitting relay points which brought them down to power the workstation, and others to end on jury rigged naked light bulbs. Kane could see why Naci wanted to go up the food chain if this was how he was living...

Kane shifted position so that not all his weight was on his wrists.

"You have in your own clumsy way caused us a lot of trouble, Gunnery Sergeant Kane. Being one step ahead of you hasn't been that hard, it has to be said, but you've certainly made what we've been trying to achieve all the more difficult."

"Traitors gotta trait."

"I see myself as less of a traitor, more of a free-lancer these days. The government we've both worked for has let us both down in a spectacular fashion."

"Yeah, but only you were trying to sell nuclear secrets to the highest bidder. Me, I just grumbled a bit."

Kohl's hissy laughter again.

"So, they haven't told you I take it?"

"Told me what?"

"That the centrifuge schematics were fake?"

Another voice. Cultured. Urbane. Deadly.

Kane turned his head. Naci Sherifi Zindashtia was leaning against a wall, peeling an orange with long, watchmaker's fingers. Kane had only seen Hennessey's surveillance shots, but it was him. "Naci. So, you are here?"

"Where else would I be when my girl Midnight tells me that she's escaped from Bagram, and got herself a fantastic asset to bring in. I've been wanting to meet you for a very long time—just not under the circumstances you would have preferred."

Focus.

"What do you mean the schematics were fake?"

Naci smiled. "They really haven't told you, have they? That's very interesting. All the squalid little battles you've fought trying to track me down, have all been for... well nothing, Gunnery Sergeant

Kane."

Kane's head was fuzzed from the beating and confused by what Naci was saying. "I don't understand."

"Well of course you don't. You're just...what do you call them...a grunt? That's correct isn't it, Kohl?"

"Indeed. Grunt. The noise a pig makes. Apt."

Naci continued. "Those schematics were leaked to Dansk precisely to see what we'd do with them, once she passed them on to us. A CIA deception and misinformation operation. To wind us up like toys and set us running. The meeting you interrupted in Tirana, where unfortunately Abdul Manani was killed, was not, as I'm sure you thought a meeting to sell the schematics to the Big Circle Boys. No, they sent us a man who could understand them. He took one look in the attaché case and almost laughed his guts up. It's a shame about Manani, but at least he got word to us before you removed him with extreme prejudice."

Kane reeled. This could be all bullshit. Bullshit of the highest order. But it wouldn't be the first time Langley had pulled shit like this, and it wouldn't be the first time Kane and his team had been put in harm's way for little or no reason.

Some might say it came with the territory. Big picture stuff that the individual pixels like Kane and Team Reaper didn't need to see all of to be in the picture themselves.

Didn't stop it hurting that little bit. Seeing Hennessey falling from the helicopter again and splashing open like a can of tomatoes fired at a wall from a hand cannon.

Focus.

Don't let this run away with you. If you're going to get out of this, revenge is not the key. Revenge is the wrong emotion. Revenge is a waste of energy.

Naci pushed a segment of orange into his mouth and chewed on the succulent and juicy fruit. A line of juice appeared to run through his beard, and he wiped it away with the back of his hand. "Baddar!"

As he'd been waiting for a signal, a boy of about twelve years ran promptly into the room. He was dressed simply in traditional dress, he knelt at Naci's feet and held up a damp towel. Naci took the towel, wiped his hands and his chin, and put it back in Baddar's hands.

Kane felt his guts tightening at the spectacle of childish submission, and the way Naci smiled down on the boy and sent him away with just a flick of his eyes.

The boy nodded and ran away, head down, out of the room.

It was one thing, Kane thought, to read and know the evil about the evil practice of *Bacha bazi*, but it was a whole other level to see it in operation. If there was any doubt that when Naci and Kohl had had their fun with Kane that they might show any mercy towards him, that notion soon flew from his mind.

Focus.

That was it. He didn't need revenge anymore. Not revenge for Hennessy or the dead and wounded of Team Reaper. He had this.

He had Baddar and his damp cloth.

CHAPTER 24

Ok. What did he know?

There were perhaps, he estimated, thirty guards at the compound who had been making ready to leave the facility, take everything with them and head for the mountains. Mountains where there were huge networks of Mujahedeen dug tunnels, which had been used to resist Russian invasion forces for years, as the Afghan fighters had fought their guerrilla war.

If Naci got there, he would be lost for good.

Satellite imagery had shown a Russian made Mi-26 Halo Heavy Transport Helicopter on the ground at the compound. It had flown in the night before according to intel, and it was large enough to evacuate the whole of Naci, Kohl and his fighters.

Something had to be done fast.

If Naci had been allowed to get to the mountains, then they would lose him for good, and revenge or no revenge, Kane would not be able to complete his mission.

Through the one window in the room, Kane could see that night was advancing across the plain. Full dark would be here in a matter of minutes, and if what he had planned was going to come to fruition, then it would not be very long until the shouts from outside the house were raised, Kohl was alerted and Kane would be shot first. And possibly Midnight second.

The razor blade concealed in the sheath belt around his waist, in the small of his back, was easy enough to get out as he lay on his hands, without arousing suspicion. He'd had to wait until they'd turned him over to do it, but now he had already sawed through the zip lock around his wrists, and the feeling was returning to his fingers.

Midnight was sitting crossed legged on the sofa. Her job, as they'd planned was a little easier to put into operation.

She'd been wary when Kane had suggested the idea to her back at Bagram where her debrief was over, and the articles of defection were in place.

She'd fought hard alongside him when Kohl had killed her lover Clark, and his lover Hennessy. Like Kane she had enough reason to want to get up close and personal with Kohl and Naci, and so the idea of her taking him zip locked and beaten had appealed to her sense of adventure, if nothing else.

The sheath belt she wore contained enough flash powder once ignited and thrown to debilitate anyone momentarily if they weren't looking away.

All they had to do was wait for the first shout from the compound.

In the end, the Halo drop Team Reaper had performed from twenty-five thousand feet, through the dark, silent as falling stars, was completed with thuds on the roof of the building and the first shots fired.

Naci and Kohl looked around. There had been nothing on the screens the boy was watching. Nothing to tell them anything had been approaching at terminal velocity.

As Kohl and Naci focused on the screen for the second they needed, Midnight whipped the charge from the sheath belt and flicked the igniter. Throwing the belt away from her like a snake, the guards didn't get a moment to even raise their weapons before the flash burned red outside Kane's closed eyes, then he was up, pulling the nine inch sprung steel belt knife from the front of his pants.

The first guard was stuck through the stomach, and the second was sliced open by Midnight's knife less than a second later as she'd leapt at him from the sofa.

Kane and Midnight bent to pick up the AK-47s the dying guards had dropped and opened up on the room.

Naci and Kohl were already gone. The boy who

had been sitting with the screens was now on his knees rubbing at his streaming eyes, as the workstation rattled, crashed and exploded as the bullets which had been meant for Naci and Kohl tore it apart.

The boy screamed and hit the floor.

"Cover the doors," Kane said as he stooped to check the boy for concealed weapons. "He's clean."

He dug the butt on the AK-47 hard into the back of the boy's skull. He'd be unconscious for the duration.

The sound of furious shooting from outside lit up the window with a dozen muzzle flashes.

"This way," Kane said, leading Midnight from the living area into the warren of corridors at the back of the house.

Someone hit the lights and the corridor was plunged into new darkness. Kane pushed Midnight to the floor and automatic fire crashed around them. If it was Naci and Kohl, they weren't going down fighting.

Kane and Midnight returned fire and the corridor sang with bullets, chewing through walls and ceilings, plaster and mud dust bursting around them in gritty clouds.

Then all they could hear was the fire fight going on outside. The double *whump* of two grenades detonating at the same time, rattled the corridor and Kane's teeth.

Nothing more came at them from the end of the corridor, and so they got up and ran on. There were skylights along this part of the house, and it threw in sufficient illumination from the moon to give them enough light to go by.

They came to a T-junction.

"Left or right?" Midnight said.

Kane ran right, and heard her soft footsteps going off in the opposite direction.

This part of the house held a set of simple wooden stairs going up to another story—he'd come through the bungalow section now. There were also five doors leading down the corridor away to a dead-end wall. There were more cables running across the ceiling, and Kane saw they junctioned off into the rooms, through rough holes that had been punched into the plasterboard walls in this, what seemed like, new section of the house.

Stairs or rooms?

Neither were the most inviting, with no flashlight and just what ambient light there was seeping in from the corridor he'd just run down. The stairs ran up into a dead gloom. None of the doors looked particularly inviting.

The battle outside the house was raging hard, and there was no way he could hear if anyone was moving about up the stairs, but that would mean no one would be able to hear him coming.

Kane would always shout at movies where the

bad guy ran away from the good guy upstairs. Going up stairs was the stupidest route to take. You'd always run out of places to go however high the building and the higher you went, the more chance there was of you not being able to leap off the building to safety without killing yourself—however good your parachute roll was.

Kohl was that kind of stupid.

Kane took the stairs.

There were thirteen wooden slats leading up to a landing, that held another set of three closed doors which Kane could see by the light from a couple of dusty windows. Kane had to duck as one of the windows blew in a gale of gunfire from outside. And then a line of bullets smashed through the thin wall and peppered the wall on the other side of the corridor.

"Gahhhh!"

Kohl's voice from behind one of the doors.

He had been that stupid.

Kane crabbed along the corridor, single shots from the AK-47 through door and wall. There was scrabbling behind one and a whispered prayer.

Kane kicked the door.

"I surrender! I surrender!"

Kohl was on his knees, hands in the air, face covered in sweat. Terror in his eyes.

"I know the rules! You can't kill me! I said I surrender!"

Kane shot him between the eyes.

"Sorry Mister Kohl, I didn't catch that."

Kohl's body fell over and begun leaking onto the rug and on the floorboards. Kohl's death tableau was lit up again by the largest explosion yet, which knocked out the last of the glass in the window behind him. Kane ducked as the slivers of it were pushed through the air by the blast.

Kane got up and cleared the rest of the rooms in the corridor.

Naci, it seemed was not that stupid. Kohl had gone upstairs, but he had not.

Kane took himself back down to the corridor. There were flames from outside showing through a trunk-sized hole in the wall, illuminating the corridor pretty effectively now.

The first door opened easily, and there was an empty bedroom beyond.

The next was the same but not empty. There were four boys in there cowering in the corner. Not knowing which way to turn.

They held up their hands, their tear stained faces glimmering in the light from the fires outside.

"Stay here," Kane said ineffectually, knowing they probably couldn't understand him anyway. "We'll be back to get you out soon. Have you seen Naci?"

Naci was a word all four did understand, and the weight of that word on Kane's heart almost snapped off the edges. One of them nodded. Pointed to the room across the corridor.

Kane nodded.

This was too close for comfort, so as quietly as he could, be motioned to the boys to get up and run along the corridor. It took him vital seconds for them to start moving, but, with the right signals and pointing the gun at the floor, so they didn't think they were going to be shot in the back—the boys left the room and ran hopefully to safety. There was plenty of firing still going on outside. Naci's guards were putting up a spirited defense, but Kane couldn't imagine they were going to hold out much longer against the skills of Team Reaper. Even if he wasn't leading the front line of the assault.

When the last boy had disappeared around the corner of the T-junction, Kane put three bullets through the door, then kicked it open, covering what angles he could as he scanned the room.

The three bullets should have sent anyone in the room diving for cover.

But in this instance they hadn't.

Naci was sitting quietly on a bed, facing the door looking like he was at peace with his world, and that his empire wasn't crashing around his ears.

Naci was unarmed. Or at least that's how he seemed.

His hands were in his lap, and as Kane raised the AK-47 to deliver the bullet he'd been wanting to deliver since the moment he'd been sent on this mission, Naci pointed to his own wrist.

"I wouldn't if I were you," he said quietly.

Kane saw the wire running from Naci's sleeve to a thumb detonator in his palm. Naci's thumb was poised over the button, and as Kane looked, the cold feeling in his stomach spreading like a fallen slush puppy, he saw the wire in the vest around Naci's torso, the pockets of the belt which would hold explosives and ball bearings, nails and bolts to cause maximum shrapnel damage to anybody in the vicinity.

"You're not going to take me alive."

"That was the idea."

"That's not what I meant. What I should have said is you're not going to be alive to take me." Naci smiled.

If Kane put a bullet in Naci's head, there was a good chance that the bomb would be detonated by reflex.

If he put a bullet in Naci's heart, he might take a second to die. Even half a second might give him enough time to press the detonator.

There was only one shot Kane could take right now and it was a complete gamble.

A roll of the dice.

He shot Naci in the hand.

Fingers flew like potato chips, blood spurted into the air and Naci howled in pain. Before he had a chance to reach the mangled detonator with his other hand, Kane aimed for Naci's forehead and pulled the trigger.

Click.

The magazine was empty.

Naci had almost reached the detonator and Kane was pushing himself backwards.

And that's when Baddar, the boy slave, who had been standing behind him fired three shots from the SIG Sauer he was holding, and gun that looked ludicrously big in his hands, into Naci's face, and the drug running, ISIS supporting scumbag, flopped back dead on the bed.

Baddar dropped the gun and began to cry.

EPILOGUE

Kane put the flowers on Barbara Hennessey's grave in the small Chicago cemetery where she'd been buried three weeks before.

He hadn't made it to the funeral, and he'd sort of been glad about that. He didn't want the questions that would inevitably come from her family and friends. Being there at the moments when she had been most alive, and when she had left her life behind, was not something he wanted to share. It was his, and his alone and he was going to keep it that way.

The roses were red and added to the vivid colors of the day. The endless blue of the sky, the dark, succulent green of the leaves, the blazing marble of the graves and shimmering emerald of the lawns.

The grave had just a simple inscription noting Hennessey's—he'd never thought of her as a Barbara—rank and how she had served her country with distinction, valor and honor, making the ultimate sacrifice.

Team Reaper had not suffered a single significant sacrifice and had taken out every single member of Naci's gang with extreme prejudice. Midnight had come back down the corridor, having found the boys coming towards her, and gone hunting for Kane.

She'd helped the sobbing Baddar out of the building as the shooting had stopped.

The helicopter was a smoking ruin, all the children were accounted for, and they set charges to raze the compound to atoms as they flew away on Little Bird with Cara.

Baddar sat with Kane the whole trip. Hugging onto his arm, refusing to let go. He'd had to be pried from the Gunnery Sergeant at Bagram Airfield, but in the end, he'd gone with the nurses to be checked over in the sick bay.

Reaper had spent nearly four more weeks with his team cleaning up as much of Naci's operation as they could. The international incident of the raid in Tirana raised, as Colonel Lord had suggested, a storm of protest in the UN, but it was a storm that soon blew itself out once the news cycle moved onto something else. The Albanians promised they would look into the corruption uncovered.

No one held their breath.

Colonel Lord wouldn't confirm or deny to Kane

the truth about the nuclear schematics. It was above his pay grade he said. He was tasked with getting them back and that's all he cared about. It didn't matter if they were a recipe for Jello florets. Orders are orders.

Kane saw things very differently, and was glad that Team Reaper, as they were, had completed the mission on the compound without a significant injury and Naci had been taken out of the game.

Midnight had asked if she could be considered for a permanent role in Reaper's team.

Kane had said he'd see.

And he would too.

When they were sure Naci's residual operations were dead and buried, the team came back to the States and Kane, as he had been itching to do, made for Chicago.

It was a windy day in the Windy City, and breezy whorls moved across the grassy lawns, shivering the trees, and gusting the leaves. Fall wasn't far away.

The only flowers he could get at the gas station were roses.

Roses would have to do.

It wasn't just a commemoration of Hennessy's life and death, but it was also a real world representation of a little of how Kane felt for the ornery CIA operative. Their time together from sparky combatants to mutual respect and to the physical embodiment of their closeness, could he felt, have led onto something stronger and deeper.

"You're being a pussy," he imagined Hennessey saying to him with that glint in her eye and sarcastic curl on her lips.

"Maybe I am," he would have said back to her if they were having this conversation for real. "But I bought you roses—from a gas station. Didn't want you to think I was going overboard."

"Ha!" Hennessey would have said if she were there, Kane was sure. "Gas station roses, you're quite the romantic, aren't you?"

"If you say so."

"I do."

Kane got up from where he had knelt to lay the roses on Hennessey's grave.

"But before you go," she might have said. "I'm not a roses kinda gal. Next time...bring me thorns."

Kane laughed and felt immediately better. He walked away from the grave, into the wind, with a broad smile on his face.

"I may well do that," he said to the sky. "In fact, I think I will."

ABOUT THE AUTHOR

A relative newcomer to the world of writing, Brent Towns self-published his first book, a western, in 2015. Last Stand in Sanctuary took him two years to write. His first hardcover book, a Black Horse Western, was published the following year. Since then, he has written a further 26 western stories, including some in collaboration with British western author, Ben Bridges.

Also, he has written the novelization to the upcoming 2019 movie from One-Eyed Horse Productions, titled, Bill Tilghman and the Outlaws. Not bad for an Australian author, he thinks.

He says, "The obvious next step for me was to venture into the world of men's action/adventure/ thriller stories. Thus, Team Reaper was born."

A country town in Queensland, Australia, is where Brent lives with his wife and son.

For more information:
https://wolfpackpublishing.com/brent-towns/

Made in the USA
Middletown, DE
22 February 2021

34186493R00175